Second Chance
COWBOY

Cowboy Hero, Book 8

BARBARA McMAHON

One

Holly Murphy reached into the back of her shiny new red Ford pickup truck and dragged the last box onto the tailgate. This one was the heaviest–it contained all the books she'd brought. Most were reference books. She preferred her Kindle for escape reading. But these were textbooks she wanted to keep handy. She paused to gather her strength before lifting it. She was dog-tired.

The drive up California's central valley, across the mountains and into the Sierra Valley had been long and tedious. She'd been on the road all day starting with the heavy morning rush hour traffic in LA. Stopping only twice, she arrived less than an hour ago in Redbud, the small Sierra Valley town near the Nevada border.

She promptly unloaded everything, stacking the boxes in the living room of the house provided for her. This was the last box. Of course, taking them off the truck didn't mean they'd been emptied. She still had to unpack and put things away. For the next six months, this would be home.

The old rambling house included the veterinarian's office, exam rooms and a small kennel in the back. Dr. Watson combined his home with his office. That made things easier. She explored the place as soon as she arrived, noting one side was the living side, the other side the office/hospital side.

There were no nearby neighbors. A plus if barking patients raised a ruckus.

All she wanted now was to get as much put away as she could before she ate, showered and fell into bed. She could sleep a week.

Wrapping up her temporary job in LA left her with mixed emotions. She'd enjoyed the companionship with the friends she'd made, but this was too good an opportunity to pass up.

For the next six months she'd be the only vet in the county. She looked forward to putting into practice all she'd learned over the last seven years.

She rubbed her hands on her faded denim shorts, blew an errant strand of brown hair from her eyes and prepared to lift the heavy carton when a battered pickup truck turned off the main road and into her short driveway, stopping only inches from where she stood.

Glad to put off carrying the last box in, she turned to watch. The engine died and the driver's door thrust open. A tall cowboy unwound from the truck and slammed the door, crossing the short distance between them smoothly, his eyes running a bold appraisal down her figure.

She bristled at the blatant assessment. Who did he think he was? Then warmth exploded through her. Holly frowned, angry at her involuntary reaction to the stranger's assessing look. Other men had done so and she'd always ignored them. Just as she'd ignore him. Or tried to.

When his expression showed interest, she suddenly felt as if she were the most attractive woman in the world.

He needed his eyes examined. She was hot, tired and dusty.

Still, it felt nice.

Not that she'd dwell on that. She was here in a professional capacity. Not to fall for some sexy cowboy. Who could be married and have six kids for all she knew.

She drew herself up to her full five-foot-two-inch height and turned back to reach for the box. If she was to have company, she wanted to go inside and didn't want to waste the trip.

"Here, darlin'", let me take that. It looks too heavy for you."

The voice drawled—no other way to describe it. Holly turned around as fast as the heavy load would allow and stared at him. Was he putting it on?

The man was rugged, muscular and lean. His shirt displayed his broad shoulders, the sleeves rolled back to reveal deeply tanned arms. A quick glance showed that his jeans were snug, worn white on the in-seams most likely from long hours in the saddle. His scruffy cowboy boots were dusty and worn.

Dragging her gaze upwards, finding his blue eyes laughing down at her while the creases near his mouth proved he smiled a lot. She couldn't see much of his hair, it was hidden by the cowboy hat which was pulled low enough to shelter his eyes from the sun.

She rolled her eyes at his comment.

"I can manage," she said, taking a step towards the porch.

For a moment, she wished she'd taken him up on the offer, the box was heavy!

"I'm sure you can, but my mother would have my hide if I let you. I'll carry it."

With no more said, he effortlessly lifted the heavy box from her hands and tucked it beneath one arm as if it weighed next to nothing.

Holly lifted her eyebrows in surprise, thought better of arguing, especially when she was relieved she didn't have to struggle with the box herself. She led the way into the house, her visitor right behind her. The box was no lightweight, yet he handled it as if it were full of tissue paper. She was impressed in spite of herself.

She also wondered how his mother would ever find out either way.

Holding the screen door, she motioned to the stack of boxes stacked neatly in the center of the small living room. "Thank you, it can go there with the rest."

He complied then swept the hat off. Running his fingers through his dark blond hair, he turned to face her. His eyes were a dark blue, almost navy, slightly amused in their regard from his lofty height. His blond hair was streaked with white. He smiled as his gaze traveled down her again, and his teeth were startling white against his dark tan when he smiled.

"Looking for the doc," he said, glancing around.

His voice fascinated Holly—deep and rich with a drawl that would have most women clamoring to hear more. She stared a moment listening to the echo of his voice in her mind.

Cache McKendrick waited while the woman seemed to be thinking. He wondered who she was and what was so hard about responding to his request for the vet. A quick glance at her left hand suggested she wasn't the new vet's wife. She wore no rings.

There was an unfamiliar tightening in his gut when he looked at her, but he ignored it. Later he'd take the time to learn who she was and why she was in Redbud–find out if she was seeing anyone and how long she planned to stay. He had more important things to deal with right now.

He sure hoped she was the doctor's sister and not his wife.

But for now he needed the doctor, not some beautiful woman no taller than his shoulder with rich, wavy brown hair, eyes the color of fine brandy and a trim figure that cried out for a man's touch.

"Doc Watson's replacement," he clarified, his gaze taking in how pretty she was and how tired she looked.

Just so he'd be able to describe her if anyone asked about her, he told himself, liking what he saw. The trim body was a cowboy's dream. The legs showing beneath the shorts tanned a honey color. The pretty shiny brown hair he wanted to touch to see if it felt as silky as it looked.

Sure, he'd like to get to know her better. But later. He needed the vet now.

"You've found me," Holly said.

Her nerve-endings tingled. She felt as if he had reached out and caressed her. His eyes were intense, his scrutiny thorough. She willed herself to remain calm and to ignore the awareness that sprang up, but her heart pounded faster and she felt warmer than she had at the blazing hot rest stops of the long car ride up.

She longed to put some distance between them, but held her ground. She refused to be intimidated by some brash cowboy. She was the interim veterinarian and the urgency in his tone sounded as if he needed her immediate services.

There was no denying the blatant sexuality of the man, from his cocky stance to the way his gaze boldly traveled over her body. He exuded confidence bordering on arrogance. He probably had women throwing themselves at him his whole life, so who could blame him? He was the most compelling man she'd ever seen.

And she was used to being around good looking men, from her uncle and cousins through to colleagues of her profession. The difference was never before had she been so physically aware of another.

She was fascinated by him–and her own reaction. Did it come from being so tired?

He frowned, his eyes narrowed and he glanced quickly around as if looking for someone else. Anyone else. He looked at her again, the laughter gone from his eyes. His face was serious his expression determined.

"You can't be. Doc Watson said he'd gotten a locum in for the time he's gone, a Doc Murphy—H. Murphy."

Holly stood as tall as she could, tilting her chin slightly, and nodded crisply.

"That's right, I'm Dr. Holly Murphy, standing in for Dr. Watson for the next six months. What can I do for you?"

"Well damnation." He said the word softly, almost as a

sigh. He shook his head, frustration showing for the first time.

"There's been a mistake, darlin'". You go on back to the city and watch out for the cats and dogs you're used to. We need a large animal vet up here. Not some pretty little thing used to Pekinese pups." His tone was disgusted.

How could someone her size deal with cattle and equines?

Holly bristled instantly. "Now hold on a minute, cowboy. Before you jump to any conclusions, you need to get your facts straight. I am a large animal vet. I specialize in cattle and equines, can handle goats and pigs and any other farm animal you can name. I'm just as good a vet as your Doc Watson."

She tilted her chin up, her eyes snapping at the implied judgment that she couldn't do the job because she was a woman. She'd been proving herself for years now and this opinionated cowboy wouldn't be the one to find her lacking.

Maybe she exaggerated a little when saying she was as good as Dr. Watson—she didn't have the years of experience that vet had. But she knew what she was doing. She'd excelled in school, was fully qualified, had been in practice for two years.

"You're not big enough," he countered, his gaze drifting over her again, lingering on the shapely legs the shorts displayed, lingering on the honey-gold of her skin, the trim ankles, muscular calves. His eyes met hers again and he shook his head.

"I'll get Stan over from Overilla."

"Who's Stan?" she asked, wondering who this cowboy thought he was to pass judgment on her abilities sight unseen.

Would she find this kind of blatant distrust throughout

the area just because she was a woman?

She hoped not. She really wanted this job.

She needed this job.

"Stan Connors is the vet over in the next county. He can help me out." He turned to go.

Holly reached out impulsively and stopped him as he was turning. His skin was warm, the muscles on his forearm tight and firm.

He wanted a vet. He had one. Her.

"Just a minute, cowboy. I'm fully qualified. What do you need, Mr…?" She trailed off. She didn't even know who he was.

Cache felt her touch on his arm, the shock of her skin against his. His eyes narrowed as he watched her. He could almost feel her determination, her tenacity, the sheer strength of her resolve as she glared up at him. For a moment he wavered. But darn, she was tiny. Petite he thought his mother would call her. Too small to be around the large animals on a ranch.

"Don't let my size fool you, cowboy. I can handle anything you throw at me," she said.

He thought about it for a moment. He could have her come out to see the fool horse and call Stan once he got home.

After she saw what she'd be facing, she'd back off. There was time. The situation was serious enough to warrant a vet, but not yet a crisis.

"I have a mare ready to foal. She's old and not due for a few more days. Today she fell. We don't know if she's injured or not. I need a vet to check her out."

He couldn't explain his capitulation, and frowned at her, not wanting to question it even to himself.

"I'll be ready in two minutes."

Holly turned and hurried to the bedroom. Flinging her heavy suitcase on the bed, she threw it open and rummaged around for a pair of jeans. Donning an old but serviceable pair, she scrambled into her hiking boots and grabbed a long-sleeved jacket. All the normal attire for working around barns and large animals. It got cool in the evenings, so she included the jacket in case the situation took a while.

She glanced around at the suitcases in the room waiting to be unpacked, and thought of the boxes in the next room. She'd have to unpack tomorrow, no telling how long she'd be tonight.

And no dinner any time soon either. She'd grab a granola bar from her stash.

Impatiently, she checked her watch. She'd only been gone five minutes. Was he still there? Or had he taken that time to disappear? She almost held her breath as she threw open the bedroom door.

He was still standing near the door, gazing at her boxes as if wondering what each contained. He looked out of place in the living room, more like he belonged to the great outdoors. He was absently turning his cowboy hat in his hands, looking as if he were trying to read the labels on her boxes from the distance.

"Ready," she said crisply, businesslike.

She knew her size often prevented people from taking her seriously. And the fact she was a woman. The long hair that waved around her face was easily tied back when she was working. She wore very little make-up--with her dark eyebrows and lashes, she needed very little. She didn't pay a lot of attention to her looks as long as she was clean and her hair was brushed.

She was more interested in becoming a good vet. Still she knew her looks and diminutive stature sometimes fooled others into thinking she wasn't up to her profession and hated that. How could she get people to see her for what she could do, not how tall she stood?

"That was fast."

He checked out her attire as she grabbed her medical bag. His feelings were mixed. The truck out front and the black satchel she carried were brand-new. He felt somewhat mollified by the obvious well-used hiking boots and jeans.

Maybe she knew what she was doing. She still seemed too small for all the work a large animal vet needed to do. And far too pretty to want to be elbow deep in muck and stuff.

In fact, she looked too small even to carry that heavy head of hair. Though he wished he could lift a strand or two of the warm brown strands to see if it felt as silky to the touch as it looked.

He scowled. Was he getting soft?

He stepped back abruptly. "Never did introduce myself. Cache McKendrick, Lone Tree Ranch. East of town."

"Cash? Is that how you pay for everything?"

She reached out a hand to shake his formally. His fingers tightened over hers. She felt the calluses in his palms. She hadn't expected the small shock the flashed through her when their hands clasped. As quickly as she could, she withdrew hers.

His smile was lop-sided, with a hint of arrogance, but the creases in his cheeks deepened and his eyes danced in amusement at her guess.

She hoped to goodness he hadn't noticed her reaction to their handshake. She was tired. Surely that was causing this aberrant reaction to the guy.

He opened the door for her to precede him from the house and pulled it shut behind him.

"No, darlin'", Cache is short for Cachon, an old family name. John Cachon McKendrick's the full name. Most folks call me Cache. My dad's called John."

"I see." She swallowed.

Was she to call him Cache?

"I'll follow you out, save you bringing me back," she said as she led the way to the vehicles. With her GPS she could find the house again no matter how far they went to get to his ranch.

"Wouldn't be a bit of trouble, darlin'," he said, giving her another grin.

"Mr. McKendrick…"

"Cache."

"Cache, then. I am not your darling nor do I plan to be, so I think you should refrain from using that endearment."

She marched straight to her pickup truck. She'd rather die than have him learn about the curious reaction experienced deep within her heart when he called her that. She'd never in her life had anyone call her darling and for a moment she wistfully wished she was someone's darling.

Straightening her shoulders, she pushed the thought away. She was doing what she'd always wanted and at the end of this assignment she'd return home at last—finally proving to her family that she could make it on her own. They'd have to accept her as a competent professional once she had some more experience under her belt.

Time enough for personal relationships after that hurdle was overcome.

"Whatever you say, darlin'," McKendrick said softly just as she reached the truck.

When she glared at him she saw his laughing eyes.

Lips tight with displeasure, Holly got into the truck and slammed the door, wondering if anyone ever got the last word with him.

Or if he took anything seriously.

Cache backed his truck out on to the road and roared away. Holly hurried after him, determined he wouldn't lose her on the way to the Lone Tree Ranch.

She needed to get a map of the area and start learning her way around, but for now she was dependent on following him. She wouldn't give him any reason to think she couldn't do the job, especially with something as simple as following him to his ranch.

His truck looked old and battered, but it obviously had a good engine because she was hard pressed to keep up with him.

She was curious about him. Her first client in Redbud. He must be doing well to own a ranch at such a relatively young age. She pegged him for around thirty. Or maybe he was just a cowboy who worked on the ranch, but because he called it home, he identified it as his ranch.

It'd been more than seven years since she'd last been home. Her lips tightened. Time enough to worry about changes later—no sense worrying about how her uncle Tyson would greet her when she did return.

She'd set out to prove herself and she'd succeeded. At least to herself.

Now she had to prove herself to her uncle. Then she'd know she made it.

The truck ahead slowed and turned on to a long, narrow graveled drive, fenced on both sides. Cache picked up speed again and Holly matched him, gravel churning, dust rising behind them.

When the buildings came into view, she spared them only a glance, following right behind the dirty truck as it drew to a sudden halt before a huge barn, dust settling softly as she pulled up beside him. There was a large corral for horses on the left of the structure and a smaller one on the right.

At some distance to the left, a long, low ranch house blended with the landscape in the afternoon light. It was set on a slight knoll, its sandy stucco walls and tile roof looking as if it had belonged to the land from the beginning.

She spared it one more glance before looking back at the barn and the corrals that flanked it. Several horses stood in both corrals, their heads raised ears pricked forward as they watch them.

She smiled involuntarily. She loved horses.

The barn was a big structure, built solid, with wide double doors left open.

Cache opened her door before she stopped looking, his expression a bit uncertain.

"You sure you know what you're doing?" he asked as Holly pulled her case from the seat beside her.

"Yes. Where's the mare?"

She hopped down and stood beside him, having to tilt her head back to see him. The brim of his cowboy hat still shaded his face, yet she could see his narrowed gaze as he stared down at her.

She needed to prove herself to this man if she wanted a successful stay in Redbud.

Shaking his head, he murmured, "I'm a fool for a pretty face." Slamming the driver's door, he turned and entered the barn. "This way."

She watched him as he walked away. Walked was such a mundane word—his movement was a smooth as a wolf's when he was hunting prey, as arrogant as a stallion's when strutting before brood mares, as unconcerned about others as she'd ever seen. Sashaying after him, she tried to emulate his rolling gait, but knew after only a few steps that she couldn't do it.

Shaking her head at her fanciful nonsense, she entered the big barn ready to prove to Cache McKendrick that she was a competent veterinarian who knew her animals.

Cache was already halfway down the center aisle. His longer stride out paced her easily. Box stalls ranged on both sides, the loft opened in the middle, sweet-smelling hay stacked high. Easy enough to feed the horses in the stalls below from the edge of the loft.

Holly noticed only a few stalls had occupants as she hurried toward the end of the aisle. Most of the horses were out in the corrals she'd seen when they first drove up. Or out working on the range, she guessed.

Two other cowboys stood by the stall that Cache walked to. They were leaning on the half door, watching an older man in the stall with the mare.

Holly didn't pause. She unlatched the half-door and slipped inside. She was the vet and had better take charge before Cache changed his mind and called the one from Overilla.

The mare was lying on her side, obviously swollen with pregnancy. The old man was stroking her neck and crooning to her when Holly squatted beside him.

"How is she?" she asked softly, her eyes taking in the situation.

She could see the swelling in her foreleg, but that wasn't causing the mare's problems. She was in labor. Early labor, if Cache's earlier pronouncement was correct.

"Who are you?" the old man asked in surprise.

"She's the new vet." Cache joined them in the stall. "Doc Watson's replacement. Is she in labor?"

Holly knew he wasn't referring to her. She ran experienced hands over the mare.

"Yes."

"I'll call Stan." Cache turned, only to be caught up again by Holly's hand firm on his arm.

15

"You go call whomever you want, Mr. McKendrick. But I'm going to help this horse. And once another vet finds out a qualified vet is on-site, he won't rush over to butt in."

She hoped that was true. What was she going to have to do to prove to this arrogant cowboy that she could do the job?

She refused to let her first assignment be passed over to someone else—she'd never be able to gain the trust of the local ranchers if she let that happen.

"You two going to jaw all day or help this poor horse?"

The old man stood up and looked over to them. Holly turned and saw that he was taller than Cache and thin as a rail. A good wind would likely blow him away. His hat covered most of the gray hair, but he wore his longer than Cache so it showed.

"I'm here to help the mare. When did this start?" she asked.

Holly was all business. She couldn't change what McKendrick might do. All her focused needed to be on helping this horse. Holly remembered Cache had told her the mare was old. Labor had started after she'd been injured. Stress would deplete her strength. She needed to deliver and be tended to before it became too much for her.

"She fell in the corral. We had a time getting her up and in here. Then she lay down again and hasn't moved," the old cowboy said.

"You're not strong enough if any heavy work needs to be done," McKendrick said to her back.

She threw him an annoyed look, running her gaze down the length of him, and knew that was a mistake. He wasn't the only one studying the opposition. For a moment she thought no one could possibly wear jeans that snug and not have them painted on. She dragged her gaze back to his face to meet his gaze.

"You've got the brawn and in this case I've the brains to know what needs to be done. You can help if I can't do it alone," she said.

She doubted he'd be needed, but if he was, she wouldn't let pride do anything to injure the horse.

Cache nodded. He watched as she examined the mare. He wondered what she'd seen when looking at him like she had. Not that it mattered. Dang, he needed to keep his mind on Sunlight. His mare needed help. He hoped to goodness Holly Murphy was as good as she said.

He was reassured to see she didn't sound so hardheaded that she'd insist she do everything herself. He didn't mind being the brawn. As long as the horse was okay.

In the meantime, he knew a thing or two about animals, too. He hoped between them they could save Sunlight. If not, it wouldn't be because he didn't give the new doctor every chance.

He hoped he was making the right decision as he went to stand beside her. He didn't want to sacrifice one of his favorite mares to have the doctor prove a point.

He wished Doc Watson were still in town.

Hours later Holly smiled tiredly at the spindly-legged foal that tottered near his mother. She leaned against the stall wall and watched him, almost too hungry and tired to move. She wondered if she could even stay awake long enough to drive home.

Yes she wasn't ready to go. She loved the new babies. It was the best part of her job.

She wasn't needed here any longer. If Cache didn't chase her out, she'd stay for a little longer and watch the new baby and his mother. She delighted in the awkwardness of his first steps, of the wonder in the colt's eyes as he took in everything for the first time.

It'd been a long session. First she'd fixed up the leg that had been injured when the mare fell. She constantly monitored her labor. When she was having trouble and the foal needed help, it was Holly who directed Cache just where to place his hands beside hers. She'd given him the directions needed as they worked together as a team to assist in the birth.

During the long hours of waiting before the birth, Cache joked with his fellow cowboys, told stories, swapping yarns between them, designed, Holly suspected, to keep his mind off the difficulty of the birth. Most of them had sounded like tall tales but they helped her feel more at ease.

It'd been a thoughtful thing to do. She glanced at Cache, wondering if her assessment of him was entirely correct. Was there more to him than brash, cocky cowboy?

And to her knowledge, he hadn't called Stan.

She smiled again and looked at the men. They didn't look as tired as she felt, thought it would soon be dawn and Cache worked alongside her the entire time. The other cowboys who had been watching were done pounding each other on the back, congratulating themselves on the new birth as if it'd been their idea. Now several still hung over the half door and gazed at the new baby.

She smiled at the mare. Where was the credit for Mama?

The horse was standing, favoring her injured leg, nuzzling her new offspring. Some of Holly's tiredness faded watching them.

Cache caught her look.

"Should give the mare credit for a little of it, right?"

She saw the lines that fanned out by his eyes, evidence of the long hours he spent in the hot California sun.

She nodded and looked away, disconcerted that he seemed to read her mind.

"She did do most of the work," she murmured, wondering how she'd find the strength to get home. She was even too tired to look at her watch. How late was it? Or how early?

"Darlin", I take back every suspicious thought I had about you. You did real good."

He leaned closer to her so the others wouldn't hear. His breath ruffled across her cheek, his eyes smiled at hers. For a second Holly wondered what would happen if she leaned forward just a little bit and let her lips brush across his.

Her eyes widened at the startling idea, heat washed through her. Were the long hours scrambling her brain? Was she so tired she'd fallen asleep and was dreaming?

She'd just met this cowboy. And wasn't sure yet if she even liked him. She stared at him, hoping her thoughts didn't show, wishing a clever retort would spring to mind. She needed to get home.

Cache's smile faded as he stared into Holly's brandy-colored eyes. She'd been here for hours, yet appeared as cool and serene as if she'd just left her place. Her skin was creamy smooth and lightly tanned like honey, her hair dark and soft, highlights glinting in the artificial light, pulled back with a string they'd found for her. He longed to release the tie and let her hair swirl about her face the way it had when he'd first seen her that afternoon. He still wondered if it felt as soft as it looked.

Abruptly he frowned and stood. Offering his hand to help her up, he asked, "Thanks, Doc, how much do I owe you?" His voice was cool, abrupt.

"I'll send a bill. I need to go home now. I'll stop by tomorrow, or rather later today, to check on them both. But I think they'll be fine."

She wouldn't leave if she thought either was in danger.

More than anything, she wanted something to eat and some sleep. She thought she was tired when she arrived at the house yesterday afternoon. That was tired. This was exhaustion.

Slowly Holly packed up the things she'd used from her kit and snapped her case closed. She still had to walk to her car and drive home. She couldn't wait to get some sleep. Taking a deep breath, she turned and smiled coolly.

"I can take you home, Doc," the old man said. His name was Sam.

Holly had plenty of time during the night to learn all their names, and a bit of what each cowboy specialized in. She didn't know much about Cache, though. Except that he could tell a tall tale with the best of them. He either owned the ranch or was the foreman. The others had a certain deference when talking with him, though for the most part, she could tell they didn't stand on a lot of ceremony.

"I'll see her home." Cache's voice was low and firm.

"Sure, whatever. Thanks again, Doc." Sam grinned at her and nodded at Cache.

"Bye for now," Holly said to the others, Tim and Larry. They'd been at Lone Tree Ranch for several years, though Sam had been there the longest. How long Cache had been there she still didn't know. Was he deliberately being vague about himself?

Not that she cared. She'd done her job which was why she'd come to Redbud. If they needed a vet, she'd be back. Otherwise, she wouldn't likely see them again any time soon.

She walked to her still shiny truck, conscious of how conspicuous it was in the yard with half a dozen dirty and banged up vehicles. It stood out like a sore thumb. Well, a few weeks around here and hers would probably be just as dusty.

She was hot, sticky and tired. It'd been such a long day. Packing last night, night before last now. Driving to Redbud. Then the delivery. She raised her hand to pull off the string she'd used to tie back her hair. She'd have to stock some scrunchies in her bag.

The ranch had installed spotlights in the barnyard and it was as light out as it had been in the barn.

The string knotted. She tugged, but nothing happened. With a sigh, she gave up. She was too tired to fight it. She'd wait until she got home and cut it off.

"Here, I'll get it loose." Cache's voice sounded just over her left ear.

She felt his fingers working the errant string, then felt the release as he worked the knot loose and let her hair spill down. She stiffened as his fingers lingered for a moment, trailing strands of her hair through them and before releasing her.

Only then did Holly realize she'd been holding her breath.

"Thank you." Her voice was soft.

She turned and leaned against the truck, her legs not as strong as she would wish.

"I can get home fine. You don't need to show me the way. The GPS got me there the first time, I know it'll do it again."

He grinned down at her. "No problem. I'll lead the way."

Her eyes narrowed in suspicion. "If I were Doc Watson, would you show him the way home?"

She didn't want any special treatment just because she was a woman. If the local ranchers thought she couldn't do the job without special treatment, they'd never call her for assistance in emergencies. She needed to succeed in this job before she could go home. It was vitally important.

Cache rested a forearm on the edge of the truck bed, his body very near Holly's. Her throat tightened. He was so close she could smell the masculine scent of him, the hay they'd been sitting on, the slightly musky smell of dried perspiration and sunshine. And the tangy scent of horse. It wasn't unpleasant. She drew in a deep breath.

"Now, darlin", I didn't have to show Doc Watson the way home "cause he was born and raised in this part of the country. But you're new and I sure don't want you getting lost leaving the Lone Tree. We have a reputation for hospitality to uphold."

"I remember–your mother. If she ever asks, I'll tell her you offered. I can make it home on my own, cowboy."

Was he doing it deliberately, getting so close she could scarcely think? His shoulders were broad. His skin was tanned. Was he that rich mahogany all over?

She bit her lip. She was acting like a giddy schoolgirl with her first crush. Definitely a lack of sleep.

Cache stared down at her for a long moment, then nodded abruptly and stood back. "Okay then, thanks again for coming."

She'd expected more of an argument, more of his sweet-talking to try to convince her that he should see her home. And to what purpose? She could find the way. It was almost a straight shot from this ranch to the edge of town where she was staying in Dr. Watson's house.

As she backed around in the yard and headed out the way she'd come in, she wondered if perhaps he'd wanted to take her home to get to know her better. To spend a little more time together.

She shook her head. Foolish thoughts. Men like him had women lined up. He wouldn't waste his time with someone like her. And especially not as she was now.

She wanted only to get home and take a shower and go to bed.

But another night she might have invited him in.

Two

When Holly at arrived home, she hoped she'd make it inside. She was dead tired. It was dark. No lights were on inside or out. She'd have to get a timer for the lights if she was going to spend late hours in barns.

She had her key out and found the lock without much trouble. Once inside, she noticed instantly that the answering machine was blinking on the desk in the small office opposite to the living room. Flicking on the light by the door, she locked up and then debated listening to the message or waiting until she'd had a couple of hours of sleep.

What if it were an emergency?

She sank into the desk chair to listen, propping her head up on her hand, elbow on the desk. She hoped it wasn't an emergency. She wasn't sure she had it in her to go out again tonight.

A soft-spoken voice let her know that Emmie Haslet had tried to reach her. She was Doc Watson's nurse and would be coming by the office first thing in the morning. She hoped Doc Murphy was settling in okay and that the house had all she needed. Some food had been left in the refrigerator and cabinets. Emmie would give her the lay of the land when she arrived the next day.

There were no other messages, so Holly gratefully erased the message and went to get ready for bed. As she ran the water for her shower, she hoped she wasn't going to have a lot of late nights. But then, animal babies like human babies didn't always arrive between breakfast and lunch. She was lucky to get this job for six months–however the hours turned out.

Dr. Watson explained his practice to Holly when she'd first interviewed via Skype for the position as locum in his absence. He and his wife were taking a long-awaited vacation. Their first one in years. For six months they planned to visit all their children, who lived in various places in the US, then they were going on a cruise to celebrate forty years of marriage.

Holly and Dr. Watson had never met in person. But they had Skyped more than once and she knew she could do the job. He, also, had seemed convinced. She beat out a half dozen other applicants.

His practice was located in the small town of Redbud, but he was on call to all the various ranches in the area. According to Dr. Watson, there were several families in town that had dogs or cats, but most of his practice centered on the animals on the cattle ranches in the county.

Emmie was his nurse, assistant, office manager and general factotum, as far as Holly could tell from his explanation. He assured Holly she could rely entirely upon Emmie to give her all the information she needed concerning the patients in the practice. The woman had been with the doctor for more than twenty years so, according to him, she knew as much as he did.

As the hot water beat down in the shower, Holly

wondered if she'd find Emmie as welcoming as Doc. Watson said.

As far as she knew, before Cache McKendrick met her this afternoon, no one in town knew the interim veterinarian would be female. Had Dr. Watson deliberately not told anyone or had the topic just not come up in Cache McKendrick's world?

Drying off, she tried to remember everything she and Doc Watson discussed. The doctor obviously knew she was a woman. She knew, however, the general expectation would be that large animal veterinarians were men. Had he deliberately kept that a secret?

All her life she'd yearned to work on Windmere Farms as a vet. To work with the horses her uncle raised and raced. Her cousins worked there. And since Holly's uncle raised her after her parents died, she'd assumed she'd have the same chance.

However, each time Holly suggested it, she'd been told firmly that it wasn't a woman's place to do that. She'd be better suited to be hostess for her uncle and let the men take care of the horses.

Her uncle sounded like he was living in the eighteen hundreds with that attitude.

She'd been the only girl in the family and tried as hard as she could to keep up with her cousins. Despite her uncle's views, she knew what she wanted and was determined to achieve it. She'd put herself through veterinary school, her uncle hadn't been willing to spend that kind of money on a profession he didn't think suitable for her.

And she'd worked a variety of positions since graduating

that enabled her to gain experience in large animal care. After six months here, she'd be ready to return home and convince her uncle she was as capable as any of her cousins.

She turned off the light and slid beneath the covers in the freshly made bed in the guest bedroom that Mrs. Watson prepared for her. It felt heavenly to lie down, stretch out and relax. She set her alarm for seven-thirty, wanting to get up early and be dressed before Emmie arrived at eight. It had been a long first day. She'd like to think about it, but sleep claimed her instantly.

When the alarm sounded, Holly's strong inclination was to shut it off, pull the covers over her head and sleep another two hours. But that thought fled when she considered she wanted to make a good first impression on Emmie.

She jumped out of bed and dressed quickly. She hoped her blue checked cotton shirt and clean jeans were appropriate attire. Should she wear her white lab coat over the jeans?

She tried it on. Throwing her stethoscope around her neck, she'd looked a physician. Yanking the stethoscope off, she left on the coat. It did give a certain air of authority.

But were they more casual in Redbud? What did Dr. Watson wear in the office? She'd worn the lab coat around the Peterson Facility, but all the vets wore lab coats there.

She shrugged out of it and tossed it on the bed. She definitely wouldn't be wearing it on visits to the ranches.

Start as you mean to go on, she thought.

She hurried to the kitchen to put coffee on.

The knock at the front door interrupted her gazing into the refrigerator. She'd have to grab something to eat in a minute. Emmie Haslet had arrived.

Holly smiled when she met Dr. Watson's nurse. Was everyone in town odd in one way or another? Emmie was even smaller than Holly. She must be seventy if she was a day.

"Well aren't you a sight, missy," Emmie said with a warm smile. She looked Holly up and down and then nodded. "You'll do. Sorry I wasn't here yesterday when you arrived. I had a tooth that was killing me so when Randy Fells said he could see me, I dashed over. He's the local dentist. You'll like Randy."

"I have coffee brewing," Holly said trying to keep up with Emmie's rapid-fire talk.

"I'll have a big cup. Then come on in the office and I'll go over what Doc left for you."

When both their coffee, Emmie led Holly to the office and reviewed the set-up with her in rapid-fire order. She went over files and how Doc liked his notes. She showed her the drug cabinet and gave her a key.

"I have one, but know better than to give anything out if Doc doesn't tell me," Emmie said.

She finished the tour showing Holly how to use the radio that Doc Watson used when visiting ranches. "No cell service through out much of the county and especially when you get into the canyon area. This doesn't work everywhere either, but has a better reach than cell phones," she explained.

"Now, I'll log in the visit you made to the Lone Tree ranch yesterday and you tell me about how the mama and baby are doing."

Holly looked at her in surprise. "How did you hear about that?"

"Oh, it's all over town. Cache sets great store by that horse and she's a bit old to be a mama, so folks were worried about her. I expect everyone's relieved you got here in time."

Holly nodded, amazed at the grapevine's sharing so fast.

"Now I didn't book any appointments until I knew for certain you'd be settled. Doc Watson usually sees walk-ins in the morning from nine to noon. Then afternoons he makes the calls to the ranches who need him. Unless there's an emergency of course. So shall I start scheduling in the morning?" Emmie said.

"Yes. So I'm still free today. I think I'll head out to the Lone Tree Ranch to see how mama and the baby are doing,"

Holly said glad to have another day to get settled. She'd unpack her boxes and then go check on her very first patients.

"Let me show you the map I brought for you. And while you're out and about, I'll show you a couple of other ranches that use Doc a lot. Thompson's and Bardwell's. They're on the other side of town from Cache's place."

Emmie had brought out a large multi folded map of the county. She pointed out the route to the different ranches and gave Holly landmarks to watch for as she gave brief sketches of the owners and the animals they owned.

"Can you give me an address and let my GPS locate each place?"

"We don't have satellite service in some areas either. It's a marvel if you live in flat land or some city, but out here, the old ways still work best," Emmie said.

"Okay. I should recognize the way at least to the Lone Tree."

"It was a good thing you arrived yesterday in time to help— her being one of Cache's favorites and Cache being so influential and all."

The mention of Cache McKendrick's name mad Holly remember his smile, the way his eyes crinkled, the deep tone of his voice. His calling her "darlin". Her heart sped up but she merely smiled. Who was Cache so influential with? All the women in town?

Emmie offered to help unpack the boxes and Holly took her up on the offer. By lunch everything had been put away and the boxes collapsed and stored in the back porch. They wouldn't be needed again for six months.

Emmie talked a mile a minute even through lunch. By the time Holly left to drive to Lone Tree Ranch, her head was spinning with names and facts and anecdotes about her future patients and neighbors.

Grateful to be alone for a little while, Holly drove the same route she'd traveled yesterday. She checked the map only twice and was confident she had the right driveway when she turned between the fields with barbed wire fence. When she'd gone only a short distance she saw the same pick-up truck, pulled off the driveway at an odd angle. Had he run off the road?

She slowed, then stopped near the truck. Cache and another man were working on the fence lining the drive just a few yards ahead of the truck. Cache's hat was low on his face, he had discarded his shirt. His shoulders and chest gleamed with a faint sheen of perspiration as he dropped a post-hole digger into the ground, worked the levers out and pulled up some of the hard clay.

Holly was glad she wore her dark glasses today. She caught her breath at the sheer masculine perfection of his muscles working as he lifted out the dirt, depositing it beside the hole. Wow.

Her cousins belonged to a health club and worked out several times a week in hopes of getting a physique like this.

They didn't even come close.

His jeans rode low on his hips, his stomach was flat and hard and ripped. His chest and shoulder muscles rippled as he worked. Poetry in motion. Only seconds after she stopped, he looked over at her. She could swear he looked directly into her eyes. With a quick word to the other man, Cache handed him the hole-digger and walked easily over to the truck.

Holly watched him as he strode towards her, the same easy gait he'd used last night, smooth, controlled, almost fluid in its grace. She nodded through her open window as he approached and gave him a polite smile. It was all she could do to stop herself from grinning like a giddy teenager.

"Howdy." Cache rested both forearms along the bottom of the window.

"Hi. I—er—thought I'd come check on my first patients. Both doing fine, I hope."

"Sure thing. Both doing fine. "Preciate your coming by, though. Might want to check on Sunlight's leg, too, see if it's healing all right."

"Yes."

She should drive on but didn't want to leave.

"Aren't you hot out here?" she stalled.

The sun blazed from a clear sky. Holly was used to the hot summers in California, but she tried not to work directly in the broiling sun. No wonder he was so tanned if he did this every day.

"Things are getting warm. After you see to the mare and foal, stop over at the house for a lemonade or iced tea," he said, smiling down at her.

She swallowed hard.

"Maybe some other time. Emmie has me on a schedule to meet some of the ranchers around so they'll feel comfortable calling on me when they need a vet. You know some might hesitate once they learn I'm female."

She threw that out, knowing that was his exact reaction.

He smiled, his teeth white and even and straight. Her eyes were drawn to his mouth and she couldn't look away.

She licked her lips drawing his attention. When his smile faded Holly felt the very air charge with something she couldn't identify. His face was shaded by his Stetson, but she saw his gaze focus on her mouth, the amusement gone from his eyes and something hot replacing it.

"Well, I guess I'll go check on Mama."

She dragged her gaze away and to put the truck in gear.

"I'll ride up with you. You can let me know if anything's wrong." Calling over to the other man, he went around the truck, opened the passenger door and slid in beside her.

Holly felt as if he filled her truck cab and sucked all the air out. She had to physically force herself to breathe. His presence seemed greater than his size warranted. She was suddenly aware of every inch of his body as she started off watching him from the corner of her eye. His shoulders almost brushed against hers. His long legs looked cramped.

"I could have given you a report on my way out," she said nervously as she drove.

"Sure. I wanted to see you in action again, darlin'."

"Still not convinced I'm qualified to provide medical services?"

He chuckled and turned halfway round in his seat, his left arm resting on the seat back, the warmth from his skin touching Holly. She could smell the slightly musky smell of perspiration and sunshine. He could have put on a shirt, she thought, swallowing hard again.

"You're sure a defensive little thing. Any remark that can be twisted around to imply you're not a good vet and off you go. Drop the chip off your shoulder, darlin', no one's challenging you here. We're glad to have someone while Doc Watson's gone."

"I told you yesterday not to call me that," she snapped, annoyed that he'd criticized her attitude. "You weren't at all sure yesterday–or happy I was here."

She knew she was defensive, but she had to be. So few people took her seriously unless she pressed the issue. Her own family didn't.

"Well, yes, ma'am, Dr. Murphy, ma'am. I'll sure stop calling you darlin'. What should I call you, ma'am?"

He was mocking her, laughing at her and Holly's blood boiled.

"Dr. Murphy will do," she said frostily.

"Yes, ma'am, Dr. Murphy."

He continued to watch her as she drove, that tantalizing grin on his face, his eyes dancing with amusement.

Holly threw him a dirty look and wished she'd hurry up and reach the barn. He rubbed her the wrong way. When she'd snapped at him she hadn't meant for him to laugh at her.

She wished for a moment that she could capture some of the camaraderie the cowboys had all displayed last night. He spoke easily to the others, why not her?

Stopping in front of the barn at last, Holly started to get out when Cache stopped her, one hand on her arm. The fingers of the other hand gently grasp her chin, tilted her face up to his.

"A word of advice, darlin'. We're kindly folks hereabout. We help each other out and rely on each other. Each person respects the other for what each of us can do. If you're a good vet, we'll find out. You don't have to stand on airs and pretensions. Doc Watson gets on fine with everyone and we all call him Doc. Or Harry, depending."

Holly tried to listen to what he was saying, but it was hard. She could feel flames licking through her at the touch of his fingers along her jaw. Mesmerized by the serious look in his eyes, the deep tones of his voice, she was hard pressed to concentrate on what he was saying. And she didn't like it when she did.

"I don't put on airs."

Just who was he to preach to her? Some cowboy who tried flirting and didn't make it.

She jerked her head from his hand and nodded sharply. "Thanks for the lecture, cowboy. I'll keep it in mind."

She knew her tone was icy, but she was mad. And embarrassed that she'd needed to be told. She wanted to make this assignment work. She didn't want Dr. Watson to regret for an instant giving her his practice while he was gone.

And she wouldn't for anything alienate his patients.

At least not the other ones. She feared it was already too late for Cache McKendrick.

Cache sat in the truck watching her walk into the barn, her back ramrod-straight, her head high. He absently wiped his hands against his jeans. He could still feel the softness of her skin on his fingertips. He didn't remember ever touching someone so soft. Her hair last night had been like fine silk, her skin today as soft as a baby's.

He growled deep in his throat and flung open the door. He refused to get caught up with Dr. Murphy. She could do her work here and move on. He didn't care. She was nothing to him but the local vet. Temporarily.

Holly's eyes adjusted to the dimmer light inside the barn as she walked down the wide center aisle. It was quiet. The few horses that had been in last night were all out.

As she approached Sunlight's stall at the back, she could hear the soft shuffling of the horse in the hay. Reaching the door, she peered into the stall her face lighting in happiness. The mare was on her feet, ears pricked forward as she watched Holly. Near her, quizzical eyes on her, the little chestnut foal balanced on his long, spindly legs.

"Saw you drive up, Doc. Came to check on our new babe,

eh?" Sam came in from the other end of the barn. Holly smiled at him, feeling almost as if she belonged–she already knew someone in Redbud.

"Yes. Both look like they're doing fine. I want to check her leg and side again."

"Shows you know what to do. Doc Watson always comes by to check up, too."

Holly nodded. At her last practice, she'd been on call for an English-riding academy in the Hollywood hills and they were much more formal than Redbud. She liked the informality she'd noted so far.

"Dr. Murphy plans to be the perfect vet, didn't you know?" Cache's voice reached her, dripping sarcasm.

Holly ignored him. She deserved it; she'd been rude to him and didn't know how to get on his better side–if he had one.

She'd do her best to ignore him from now on. If she didn't say anything, she wouldn't give him ammunition for more teasing.

"Now, boss, she's a right smart doc, for a woman," Sam said.

Holly noted the backhanded comment as she swung around to face Cache.

"Are you the foreman of this place?" she asked trying to get a clear picture. He'd mentioned both his mother and father since she'd arrived. Though she hadn't seen either one, maybe he was running things while they were traveling like Dr. Watson and his wife were.

"Nope," Cache said.

Sam chuckled. "Nope is right. He owns the Lone Tree, Doc."

Holly stared in disbelief at Cache. No wonder he was arrogant. From what she'd seen, the Lone Tree was a large and prosperous ranch. How did some cowboy at his age get such a prosperous ranch? She'd thought him arrogant because of his good looks and physique. He could strut around all over if he owned all this.

Emmie was right—the owner of this ranch would be influential in the community. Now Holly knew where— everywhere!

"Make a difference, Dr. Murphy?" His voice was silky, his smile sardonic.

His tone fired her anger again. He was the most exasperating man!

"No. Why should it? I'm still a vet and you're still the most arrogant, brash, outrageous cowboy I've ever met."

Cache roared with laughter at her obvious frustration.

Sam chuckled and looked back and forth at the two of them.

She wasn't amused. Holly eyed Cache with hostility but prudently kept quiet. When he'd settled down to a chuckle, she gave him another dirty look and opened the stall door gently so not to spook either one inside the stall.

Checking the mare and the foal quickly, she was satisfied that both were doing well. The leg wasn't swollen any more. She suspected a bruise where the mare had fallen, but couldn't spot one through the coat. Happy the mare had come through the delivery fine, Holly had no reason to stick around.

She remained self-conscious with Sam and Cache standing by the door, watching her, however. Neither spoke while she checked her patients. When she finished, she looked at Sam, ignoring Cache.

"I'd say by tomorrow you can let them into the corral, as long as you keep them separated from the other horses for a while."

She was only saying that to cover all bases. She knew these experienced ranchers knew what to do. Same as her uncle always seemed to anticipate whatever the vet told him.

"Sure thing, Doc," Sam said, looking from Holly to Cache. "Be seeing ya." He tipped his hat and walked away.

Holly let herself out of the stall, trying not to meet Cache's eye.

How was she to know he was the owner of the ranch? In her limited experience ranch owners were in their fifties, not thirty something. He could have mentioned it.

He was frustrating enough to drive a saint crazy and she was no saint.

"Thank you, Dr. Murphy, for taking time to check on Sunlight." His voice dripped sarcasm, as he turned to match her steps.

"Don't call me that!" she snapped, knowing he was deliberately goading her, yet unable to stop the flash of anger he evoked.

"Don't call you this, don't call you that. Do you know what you do want to be called?" he asked as they headed towards the bright sunshine spilling into the barn from the large double doors, their steps muffled on the packed earth.

She didn't answer. Mostly she didn't want him to call her anything. She wanted to leave.

"Well, I know what I want."

Before she could think of a reply, he pulled her to a halt and his head blocked the sunlight from her as he swept off his hat, leaned over and kissed her right on the mouth.

His mouth was hot and firm against her lips, not dominating as she would have expected, but coaxing, tantalizing, enticing. His lips moved against hers gently, yet every second proved more exciting than the previous one. Time stood still and bright sunlight danced against her lids as her pulse beat a rapid tattoo through her veins.

Holly never tried to resist—it was too much. She softened her lips and returned a kiss of her own. The sweet smell of the hay, the bright warmth of the sunshine spilling around them, the solid feel of the half-clad body beside her filled her senses. Her free hand came up and rested against his arm. She could feel the muscles tighten beneath her fingers, the hard strength, the warmth radiating from his skin.

When he drew back slowly, reluctantly, she wanted to stop him, clutch him against her. But she stood still, silent. Slowly she opened her eyes. She saw the hot blaze of his eyes staring down at her, all traces of amusement gone.

"Know what you want yet, Dr. Murphy?" he asked, his voice soft and low, his eyes narrowed slightly.

Before she could reply, she heard a pickup truck pull into the yard. Cache straightened and slammed his hat back on his head, striding purposely towards the truck.

Holly followed slowly watching him warily. What was his

hurry? A kiss was fine, as long as no one else knew?

Well, she didn't want anyone knowing either!

When Holly reached her truck, she saw Cache in deep conversation with the man she'd seen him with earlier working on the fence. Cache seemed to know when she came into the yard for he looked up, turning to lean insolently against the dusty truck as he continued talking with the man, his eyes tracking her.

Feigning a disinterest she didn't feel, Holly tossed her head and opened the driver's door. Once safely inside, she donned her dark glasses. She felt protected, sheltered with them on. Glancing once at Cache, she saw he still stared at her.

She started the engine and gave a careless wave, proud of herself for the gesture. She turned and then watched him from her rear-view mirror as she slowly pulled away and headed back down the drive. He stared after her until the slight bend in the driveway hid him from view.

"Whew!" She let out a pent-up breath. She felt drained, as if she'd run a mile or more. What was it about that arrogant, brash cowboy that fascinated her so much?

She'd met his kind before, all her years growing up around race horses. She knew the type. Cocky men who though they were a gift to women. Even her cousin Cord acted that way. She didn't get it.

Cache seemed to back up the act with real accomplishments. The Lone Tree Ranch gave every evidence of being a prosperous enterprise. Emmie had spoken highly of it and of Cache. Holly suspected the older woman of trying a bit of matchmaking when suggesting this morning that Holly should be sure to make a return call. Maybe she was genuine in her admiration of Cache and what he'd done. And she knew to make a good impression the new vet needed to be on top of her game.

Holly checked her notes then found the Thompson ranch without any difficulty. She introduced herself to Mrs. Thompson when she came to the front door. Her husband, Holly found out, was out on the range and not expected back before supper time. But Mary Thompson insisted Holly come in for a visit and some tea. She seemed delighted to have a visitor. And was equally certain her husband would find it really interesting to have a female vet.

She'd already heard that Holly had helped the old mare deliver her foal.

Holly told her a bit about the birth and how much she loved newborn babies of all species.

"Cache sets a lot of store by that mare. I'm glad you got that baby delivered safely. I'll tell Brad when he gets back. Anyone good enough to work for Cache will be good enough for my husband. Tell me more about this new baby colt. They are the sweetest things all gangly and uncoordinated."

Holly enjoyed her visit. And the short visit to the Bardwell ranch as well.

Feeling she was starting to find her way, Holly drove into town. Redbud was a small western town, one main street with an assortment of wooden buildings, stucco and brick. None of the buildings were taller than two stories. And the mixture of colors showed a lack of cohesive planning for Main Street.

She stopped to pick up a few more items from the small

supermarket at one end of Main Street. As she drove out of town, she noted a couple of other shops she'd like to visit.

When Holly reached her house, Emmie had left for the day. Finding a note tacked to the front door, she read that Emmie would return in the morning. There were only a few calls and Emmie had left a list of places Holly should visit the next afternoon.

Letting herself into the cool house, Holly realized how hot it was outside. She was glad for the cooler air. The house had been shut up so blocked some of the day's heat.

She poured a large iced tea from the pitcher Emmie had left in the refrigerator and read the notes Emmie had left on the desk.

The phone rang.

"Dr. Murphy," Holly answered crisply.

"Just wanted to make sure you got home okay, darlin'," a familiar voice drawled in her ear.

She gave a silly grin–butterflies instantly churning in her stomach. The sound of his voice could make her forget everything.

The memory of the kiss in the barn crashed around her.

"Thank you, I did."

Was that her voice, that soft, almost beguiling tone? She shook her head. She should be mad at him for kissing her. Instead, she leaned back in her chair and sipped her tea.

"There's a dance in town next Saturday. A bit fancy and a lot of fun. Would you like to go with me?" Cache asked in that lazy don't-give-a-darn tone he had.

Holly's intent after today was to put plenty of distance

between herself and this cowboy. She couldn't afford to get involved. She was the temporary vet and didn't want anyone thinking she was looking for favoritism from anyone.

Oh but she was tempted. If she could forget how her senses scrambled when he was around. How her heart pounded merely thinking about that kiss. How he exasperated her to no end.

"I don't think so," she said slowly, reluctant to refuse, yet knowing that it'd be best for her own equilibrium. He'd probably spend the entire evening poking fun at her. She tried to rationalize her refusal.

"Suit yourself. If you change your mind you know where I am, Dr. Murphy."

"Don't call me that," she said sharply.

He did it just to annoy her and he succeeded every time.

"You're sure a gal for saying don't. Bye, Doc." With that he hung up the phone.

The minute she hung up, she wished she'd said yes. She hadn't been out dancing in a long time. And it'd be a nice way to meet people whom she wouldn't necessarily meet otherwise.

Maybe she'd been hasty, but in the long run, it would be better to stay away from Cache.

The next two days were busy. Emmie's recommendations had her visiting different ranches throughout the county— meeting the owners, meeting some of the cowboys and seeing sick animals, from horses and cattle to one little girl's pet rabbit.

The only saving grace was no emergencies and no night calls.

She didn't see Cache McKendrick, nor any of his cowhands, but she thought about him a lot. At odd moments when she'd be driving his lazy grin would spring to mind. Or when writing up her notes for the files, his sexy voice would echo. She'd remember his lopsided smile, his hat pulled low, or remember the strong shoulders and the way his muscles rippled as he worked on the fence. The way they felt beneath her fingertips.

Or worst of all, how his mouth felt against hers.

And that was the hardest memory to ignore. She knew better than to flirt with the man. But maybe just one more kiss–somehow, somewhere, some day.

On Thursday she returned home around three. It had been a light day. She headed directly for the office and the files that awaited. She kept up with the client records on a daily basis, no matter how tired she was. Today she finished early and looked forward to a relaxing evening–if she got no emergency calls. She was learning to quantify her life like that.

Emmie greeted her upon her return.

"You're back early. Get old Tom's sow fixed up?"

Holly's last call had been to look after a sick sow for one of the furthest ranches in the area.

She smiled and nodded. "For the time being. Mr. Poplar sure is attached to that pig," she murmured taking the file from Emmie and sitting at the desk to jot down her notes.

Emmie laughed softly. "He's crazy about that critter. Ever since his wife died, that pig's become his family. He'll take it hard when she dies."

"That won't be for a while yet," Holly said. "She's in good health, if he keeps her from the chocolate."

"I wondered if that was what was wrong with her. She's gotten into chocolate before."

Holly scanned the file. There were two other notations similar to hers from Dr. Watson.

"There's a dance in town on Saturday," Emmie said, studying the young vet, as she sat in her own chair at her smaller desk.

Holly kept her eyes firmly on the notes she was reading, the memory of Cache's invitation jumping to mind. She already regretted refusing a dozen or more times over the last couple of days.

"Be a shame to miss it," Emmie added, fixing her pale blue eyes on Holly.

Holly looked up. "Hmm?" she said, stalling.

"You should plan to go to the dance on Saturday. That'll give you an opportunity to meet more people, some young people. Find a few friends you can hang out with so you'll feel more at home here," Emmie said firmly.

She might be tiny, but her personality was forceful and her energy level high. "You don't want to only hang out with me and sick critters."

"Maybe I'll go. Actually, I did get asked, but I turned him down."

She toyed with the pen, refusing to meet Emmie's eyes. She'd have to find out where it was and what time. She could use the excuse she never knew if she'd be called out to show up by herself.

Emmie's eyebrows raised as she stared at Holly, the question unspoken, yet loud between them. Holly glanced at her. The silence stretched out. Holly grimaced slightly.

"If you must know, it was Cache," she told the older woman.

"Cache McKendrick asked you to the dance and you turned him down?" Emmie stared at her for a second in astonishment.

Holly nodded.

"Child, I can't remember the last time Cache asked anyone to anywhere. He usually attends events, flirts up a storm with every woman there, but he's never brought anyone, never took anyone home since Trish. And he asked you to the dance?"

Holly nodded reluctantly. Who was Trish?

"Laws, he's one of the most prosperous ranchers in the county, he and his dad are big in the cattleman's association. Hmm, and you turned him down?"

"It doesn't mean anything. He was just trying to rile me," Holly said defensively.

"Rile you? What for?"

"I don't know." Holly looked away.

She didn't want to go into everything with Emmie. It was bad enough that she had to remember what she'd said and Cache's reactions. She didn't need everyone else knowing about it. The last thing she wanted for her six months" stay was gossip running rampant.

Emmie sat for a moment, deep in thought. Finally she stood up and moved to get the phone and plop it before Holly.

"Call him now and say you'll go," she ordered.

"I can't do that."

She'd had more moments of regret over the last few days that she'd turned him down than she could count. But she couldn't call him back and say she'd go with him.

What if Emmie was wrong and he'd already asked someone else? She'd die of embarrassment.

"You can and will. It's the best opportunity you'll ever get to meet everyone in town with the backing of one of the McKendrick's. And you'd have the stamp of approval not everyone gets. You're a fool if you don't make the most of this opportunity. Doc Watson would."

"Doc Watson would have gone with Cache?" Holly asked, with a shocked look on her face, knowing she was putting off the inevitable.

"None of your sass, girl, call him now. I'll leave, so you won't be self-conscious." Emmie swept regally from the room. "Mind you call right now," closing the office door with a final order that made Holly actually consider calling him.

"Who's Trish?" Holly called after her. But there was only silence. Had Emmie heard her?

Holly stared at the phone. Dare she call?

Dithering, she wondered what she could possibly say. And how he'd react.

Stretching out the time, she slowly looked up his number and stared back at the phone. Chances were that he'd be out somewhere and not anywhere near his phone.

If she were going to call, now would be the best time. He wouldn't be there and she could tell Emmie she'd tried. She could always go to the dance alone. Meet people by herself.

That settled in her mind, she dialed the number wondering if she could hang up after only a few rings or if she should at least let it ring a long time for show.

Three

Cache answered the phone on the second ring. Holly froze. She hadn't expected him to be there at all! For a moment her mind went blank, panic swept through her. She wiped one hand along her jeans, wishing she dared hang up.

"McKendrick." His deep voice hadn't changed.

She closed her eyes, immediately transported back to that morning in the barn. She could feel his lips on hers, the smell of hay and sunshine and male scent flooding her senses. She opened her eyes, blinked and took a deep breath.

"Hello, Cache? This is Holly Murphy," she began. If he said anything to set her off, she'd hang up on him, no matter what Emmie said.

"Hello." His tone was soft, non-threatening.

"How are you?" she asked, stalling. She didn't know if she could go through with this. What if he laughed at her again? What if he'd asked someone else?

"Doing fine, and you?"

If she wanted to play proper he'd apparently play by her rules, this time. Amusement started creeping into his tone, however. She could hear it over the phone line.

She frowned—it was now or never. She didn't think she wanted to answer the inquisition she was sure Emmie would give her if she didn't follow through. The worst he could do would be to say no. She'd say she understood and then hang up.

"Er—you mentioned if I changed my mind about the dance I should call you. I would like to go, if it's still all right?" She said it all in a rush.

Too fast. Darn, why couldn't she be calm and collected and a bit aloof like the society women her uncle associated with?

"That's very much all right, darlin'. I'm glad you can make it. I'll pick you up around seven."

"Okay."

She almost sagged with relief. He hadn't laughed at her. And he still wanted to take her.

She smiled as a small bud of happiness blossomed within. Suddenly she didn't want to hang up, but she couldn't think of anything else to say. She wasn't usually tongue-tied. She could discuss cattle and horses and ranching and racing with the best of them. What was it about this man that made her so nervous and unsure of herself?

"See you then, Doc." There was definite amusement in the tone now.

Holly nodded, then realized he couldn't see her. "See you then, goodbye."

She hung up slowly, a stupid grin on her face. She was going to the dance and with Cache McKendrick, a man who usually didn't even take anyone to town affairs. Since Trish.

Who was Trish?

The date didn't mean anything. She was going to the

dance to meet people. Make a few friends she could hang out with during the next few months.

Holly was still grinning when she went to let Emmie know what happened.

"Well?" that woman asked as Holly joined her in the kitchen.

"He'll take me," she said in an offhand manner.

Even as she said it, Holly felt a warm spurt of anticipation. When she met Emmie's eyes, it was all she could do to refrain from laughing aloud with glee.

"You're right. It's a good opportunity to meet others who live in the county. Make some friends." And find a place for her to feel like she belonged, even if only temporarily.

"Right and you get to spend the evening with Cache McKendrick. I'm not so old I don't know what going with that boy will be like. Do you know we're out of liniment?"

Holly blinked at the change of topic.

"And?" Was that critical?

She wanted to hear more about what Emmie thought it would be like going out with that boy. She grinned again. Cache was no boy, he was a man through and through.

"Usually Doc Watson keeps liniment on hand, so he'd have it if that's all that's needed when he gets called out. He gets it over at Frank's Feed Store, on the far side of town. I should have noticed before so you could have gotten some when you were out."

It appeared the topic of the dance was forgotten.

"I'll stop in tomorrow and pick some up. Did Dr. Watson have a preferred brand?" Holly asked.

"Just get what you think's good."

Holly finished writing up her notes and replaced the files back in the appropriate drawers after Emmie left. The rest of the day–such as it was–was hers. She gazed through the office window into the afternoon sunshine, wondering what Cache was doing.

Working, she was sure. A man didn't build up a successful ranch lolling around.

Like she felt she was doing. Was business always this slow or were people still not sure about her abilities.

Darn, she forgot to ask Emmie who Trish was.

The next afternoon, after visiting a small homestead with three horses that needed to be tube wormed, Holly headed for town and Frank's Feed store. Parking her truck in the shade of one of the trees near the large barn-like structure, she wandered inside.

The left half of the cavernous space was full of shelves and display items from dog leashes to hoof polish, cowboy boots to bird feeders. The right wall was open to the outside and alfalfa hay and red oat hay was stacked high with a forklift out in the parking area to get down the bales when needed. Wood chips, 100 pound bags of rabbit food, dog food and an assortment of bird seeds filled the area. The scent of hay permeated the entire space. Dust mites danced in the sunshine coming in through the open wall.

She walked along the aisles carrying animal sundries. Hoof black, saddle soap, fly sprays, dozen of products for the care and well being of animals. She scanned the items as she walked. Brand names as familiar to her as toothpaste leaped out. She smiled as if recognizing old friends. So many of the brands of liniment, neat's-foot oil and saddle soap were ones her uncle used when she had been growing up at Windmere Farms. Probably still did.

There, near the bottom, Old Tom's. She knelt down to take one of the bottles and read the label. It brought back such memories—working with the grooms on the horses, mucking out stalls for the privilege of riding Blue Boy or one of the other horses. Trying it out on her own ankle when she'd fallen that time.

Memories flooded. She missed home! For a moment tears filled her eyes and an ache started in her chest. It was a self-imposed exile, but it didn't make being homesick any easier.

"Howdy, Cache, how are you?" the booming voice of the proprietor called across the store.

Holly froze, clutching the bottle of liniment, memories vanishing instantly. Blinking her eyes rapidly, she listened to hear if it was Cache McKendrick. Though how many men named Cache would there be in a town the size of Redbud?

"Howdy, Frank. Came to pick up some of that grain you and I discussed."

She'd recognize that low, lazy voice anywhere. Holly could hear them clearly, though they were probably two or three rows away, where the store opened out to where Frank had hay alongside barrels and sacks of grain and bagged wood shavings. She stayed where she was, the liniment bottle forgotten as she listened.

"I put a dozen sacks aside for you. Thought one of the boys might come to pick it up. You in town for long?"

"No, just came to get that. Wanted a break from paperwork. That'll be what drives me out of ranching one day, the blasted paperwork."

Frank chuckled. "That'll be the day, not after all you've done on your place. Want to back in your truck? I'll load it up."

Just then the phone rang. Holly heard Frank hurry to answer it. Where was Cache? Going to get his truck? She debated standing, seeing if he was around. She could at least speak to him–that would only be polite.

Her heart sped up at the thought. What would she say?

Maybe it would be better if she didn't see him. He'd be by to pick her up for the dance at seven tomorrow. That would be soon enough.

Her legs were getting a bit tired of squatting by the lower shelf. She should have stood before. She wasn't sure what to do now. Maybe he'd hurry up and pay and leave and never see her. The longer she waited, the more awkward it would be if he saw her there.

"Well, if it isn't Cache McKendrick. I haven't seen you in ages."

The purely feminine voice Holly heard most certainly wasn't Frank.

Her legs were screaming. She couldn't stand it any longer. If she didn't want to end up plopping on the dusty floor, she had to stand. Slowly she rose. The shelves were too high for her to see anyone. She stood still a moment, debating whether to walk toward the counter in the back and buy her liniment and risk Cache seeing her or remain where she stood.

"Hello, sugar. I've been around, where've you been? Hello, Joe."

"Cache. Brought this minx in to help me with some shopping. Heard Sunlight foaled. Doing okay?"

So the woman was with someone. Holly glanced around, hoping no one else came into the store.

"Yeah. Came early, though," Cache said.

"Had the new vet out to assist, I understand."

Holly wondered who Joe was. And the woman with him that Cache called sugar.

"Yep."

Holly stood still, holding the bottle, holding her breath. She wouldn't make her presence known now for anything. She strained to hear better.

"What's she like?" Joe asked.

"Seems competent," Cache replied.

Holly frowned. That was that all he was going to say?

"I don't care about that. What I want to know is if you're going to the dance tomorrow, Cache."

It was the woman again. Holly wondered what she looked like and who she was. Joe's wife maybe?

"Sure, sugar, aren't you? Save me a dance."

"You can have every one, if you want."

The flirtatious tone of her voice convinced Holly she and Joe were not married. At least she didn't think a man would put up with that right in front of him if she were his wife.

"And have every man in the county after me? No, thanks.

One dance will do me," Cache said.

Even from that distance, Holly could hear his teasing tone.

"Surely you aren't going to let other people's opinions scare you off." Her voice was definitely flirtatious.

Holly strained to hear what his response would be.

He chuckled. "She's dangerous, Joe, you'd better watch her."

"I know. If I can get her married off I'd be a happy man."

"Dad!"

Holly wondered if "sugar" and her dad would like her to marry Cache.

Not that it mattered to her.

"Come on, Sally, Frank's finished his call and I want to catch him before he starts doing something else. See ya, Cache."

"I'll save you a slow one tomorrow night, Cache—"

The woman's voice trailed off as Holly heard them walking across the wooden floor. She could follow their footsteps as they walked to the back and the sales counter.

She replaced the old liniment. If she hadn't been caught up in old memories she might have chosen her liniment and been out before Cache ever showed up. She picked up a bottle of the kind she normally used. She held back, watching the couple at the counter. She'd wait a moment and as soon as they left, she'd buy it and be on her way. No need for anyone to know she'd been there.

Anyone meaning Cache McKendrick, of course.

"Hello, darlin'." Cache came around the side of the aisle

and stopped in surprise when he saw Holly.

His hat was pushed back from his forehead and she could clearly see his blue eyes.

She glanced up immediately flustered. What would he think if he realized she'd overheard their conversation?

"Hi."

She looked back down at the bottle she held in her left hand, the fingers of her right hand rubbing against the label. She tried desperately for something to say, but nothing came to mind. Why couldn't she casually discuss the weather? Or ask after the mare and foal?

Say something, Holly!

"You're going to wear off the label if you keep doing that."

His hand came out to cover hers, pulling it away from the bottle. His grip felt warm, strong, firm, yet tender as he held her fingers.

She almost dropped the bottle. She chanced another look at him and found his eyes on her, the corners of his mouth turned up in a lop-sided smile.

Holly could scarcely breathe. She felt confined. The store was no longer big and spacious but small, crowded and stifling. Or was it just because he took up so much space? Or just took the breath from her?

He oozed sex appeal. From his tipped back hat, to the blue shirt and faded jeans, he was hot, hot, hot. It was overwhelming. She was instantly exquisitely conscious of the feelings that flooded.

She wanted to be independent, on her own, able to hold

her own in any situation. Not wondering if some man found her attractive. Not longing to find conversation that would entertain. Or check if her hair was still brushed.

His thumb began tracing lazy circles on the back of her hand. Holly could feel the reaction throughout her whole body. She seemed in tune with the motion, yearning for more. She tried experimentally to tug her hand free, but he refused to let go.

"Don't let me keep you," she said. The sooner he left, the sooner she could.

"You should have come and been introduced. Though you'll meet Joe and Sally at the dance." His mocking tone told her he absolutely realized she'd heard every word.

She looked away, trying again to pull her hand away. Wanting to put distance from this man before she did or said something really stupid.

"You going to buy that from Frank? Come on and I introduce you. Doc buys all his supplies here," Cache said, glancing again at the bottle gripped tightly in her left hand.

"I may want a few more things."

She wasn't going over there now, with everyone still there. Nor was she going to cross this store with her hand in Cache's.

"Could you let me go?" she asked politely, her gaze on his chin. She was afraid to meet him eye to eye.

"Sure thing, darlin'. For now."

She sighed as he let her hand go. "I thought I told you…"

"You're always telling me something. Tell me what you're going to wear tomorrow night," he said.

She frowned, considering. She didn't have too many

dresses. The fancy wardrobe that had been suitable for any occasion still languished back in her bedroom in Kentucky. Jeans were the most suitable clothes for her work.

Since she didn't date much, she didn't have much need for a lot of dress up clothes. Money had also been a concern since she'd been at the university. She darted a quick glance at him, looked away. She wanted to look nice on Saturday, but she had limited choices.

"I have a nice blue dress I plan to wear," she said finally. "I don't have a lot of dressy clothes. I'm more of a jeans kind of person. How dressy is this dance?"

"I thought all women had closets spilling out with dresses and things. Did the clothes gene miss you?"

That teasing he was famous for showed clearly on his face. His eyes danced in amusement as she shifted nervously.

"You didn't tell me how dressy the dance is."

It wasn't any of his business whether she went shopping all the time or not.

He smiled at her, his eyes drifting down the front of her blouse, back to meet her eyes, sparkling as her obvious irritation built. How dared he peruse her as if she were some prime horse he was considering purchasing?

"Dressy for here is probably not dressy for a big city. I'd think you'd have a ton of clothes to go with all occasion."

Cache loved watching her flare up. Her eyes flashed sparks, he almost felt singed. She stood so straight, as if trying to stretch out her brief height. He smiled at her as she searched for something scathing to say to him, anticipation building as he awaited her words.

"You sure are nosy," she muttered, turning to walk towards the counter, wishing she could think of something clever to say to wipe that amusement from his eyes.

Maybe she should change her mind again. Calling him back to say she'd go had been a mistake. He'd probably never let her forget that.

"You're being downright un-neighborly, darlin'."

His hand was gentle on her arm as he stepped in front of her, his other hand going to cup her chin with his warm fingers.

For one shattering moment she thought he would kiss her again right smack in the midst of the feed store. For one shattering moment she yearned for him to do just that.

She held her breath.

"Cache?" Frank's voice called from the back.

"We'll pick this up later," Cache promised, tapping her lips with his finger.

Then he turned to wave acknowledgment.

Holly stared after him as he walked away. Her skin tingled from the imprint of his hand along her jaw, the caress of his fingers along her cheek. The suggestive touch of his finger against her lips. She stared after him for long minutes, waiting for her body to calm down.

He was hot, sexy and definitely dangerous. She'd do better to stay far away from the man. He was more than she was used to, more than she could cope with. She knew he was only playing with her, toying with her because she was so transparent and easy to rile. But she couldn't seem to help herself.

Why hadn't she been born knowing how to flirt and tease and walk away heart-whole?

That was what her uncle thought she should practice—the gentle art of flirtation, not veterinary medicine.

It was obvious that Cache had been born knowing all the nuances of flirting. She wished she could keep up.

Scowling, she hurried to pay for the liniment and seek the safety of her truck. She saw a blonde woman in the distance with an older man. Sally and Joe no doubt. Obviously Cache was well liked by one other woman in town. Make that two, Emmie thought he was special. Holly had no difficulty believing he'd be sought after by every woman in sight.

It was odd, then, that he never took anyone to the town events as Emmie said. Was he dedicated to playing the field? No, then he'd take a different woman to every event.

She needed to ask Emmie about Trish and why Cache didn't take other women to events.

And if that were the case, what would everyone think when he arrived with Holly?

Saturday wasn't the leisurely day Holly hoped for. She'd planned to get ready in plenty of time to greet Cache with all the serenity she could muster.

Instead, late in the afternoon, she went into surgery when one of the dogs from a ranch beyond the Lone Tree was brought in badly torn up by barbed wire.

"Got tangled in a forgotten roll, struggled to get out."

The young cowhand who brought in the dog was

distraught. It was his dog and Holly knew he was scared for him. There was blood all over the dog and the man.

"Can you save him, Doc?"

"I'll do my best," Holly said, starting to prep as she lifted the dog onto one of the exam tables.

"I didn't know you were an O.R. nurse as well," Holly said as she scrubbed up. Emmie right beside her.

"Never had any formal training. Doc Watson taught me all I know. But I raised a parcel of kids. They took scrapes and cuts to a new level," the older woman said.

Many of the cuts were superficial, though there were a couple on his legs that were deep and serious. Holly spent over two hours suturing and cleaning the dog up. Emmie worked right alongside her. The procedure was not particularly difficult, just tedious and time consuming.

When she was finished, she went to reassure the owner.

"He came through the procedure fine," she told the cowboy who had waited impatiently in her office while she took care of his dog. "Some of the cuts were pretty deep. And he's lost a bit of blood, but I think he'll be just fine. You saved his life by bringing him in so fast."

"Gosh, thanks, Doc. That ol" dog means a lot to me."

The cowboy stood, twisting his hat around and around in his hands. He looked so young. Holly didn't say anything but she was sure she saw tears in the young man's eyes.

"Then you shouldn't have left the barbed wire lying around," Holly said, rubbing her back.

She was tired. A quick glance at her clock showed her she only had twenty minutes before Cache would arrive to pick her up.

"You're right, Doc. We took care of that bunch. But there's always wire all over the range. You just have to watch for it, ya know? Thanks a million, Doc. Can I see him?"

Holly smiled and nodded. "He's just waking up so will be really groggy. But I'm sure he'd like to see you. I'll keep him here a couple of days, until I know he'll fully recover. Then you can take him home."

As he hurried off to see his dog, she hastened to get ready.

She jumped in and out of the shower and was just tying her still damp hair back when Emmie knocked on her bedroom door and stuck her head in.

"Cache is here. And he looks grand. So do you."

She smiled at the picture Holly made, still in her robe, her hair clean and shining, pulled back from her face to cascade in waves to below her shoulders. She'd applied make-up with a light hand and was ready to slip on her dress.

"I'll be out in a minute."

"I'm taking off, myself. That dog's settled and young Brian's heading back to the ranch. He'll be by in the morning to see the dog. So I'll see you at the hall. Have fun tonight."

Holly nodded picking up her lipstick. Her hands shook. She was nervous. Just on the other side of that door was the man who annoyed her more than any other.

And excited her more as well.

She smeared the lipstick, wiped it off and tried again. Getting it right at last, she went to the wardrobe to get her dress.

The knock at her door stopped her. Before she could

answer, it opened and Cache peered around.

"You sure are slow."

He ran his eyes over her, noting how the robe hugged her slight frame, the deep V caused by the lapels, the soft swells of her breasts the robe displayed. "You need any help?" His voice was husky, seductive.

For once the amusement was missing and Holly found the dark blue glitter in his eyes far more disturbing. She stared back at him. He wore a dark suit, a crisp white shirt and a silver and gray tie. He looked sophisticated, cosmopolitan and downright sexy.

She'd seen him in old tight jeans, with and without a shirt, and now this. She caught her breath. He was gorgeous.

What was he doing taking her out? Any woman in town would be eager to go with him.

She couldn't look away, just gazed back at him, mesmerized by the look in his dark blue eyes, mesmerized by the pull of attraction that threatened to overwhelm her. Aware of the deep bronze of his tan, the faint lines radiating from his eyes, the white of his teeth as he smiled at her.

Holly blinked and broke contact. She took a deep breath, disturbed by the look in Cache's eyes as his gaze dropped to the opening of her robe when she breathed in.

"I don't need any help, thank you," she said breathlessly.

He nodded and smiled again, that teasing, arrogant smile that caused her heart to flutter, and warmth to spread to every cell. He was the most attractive man she'd ever seen. And she suspected he knew it.

"Just wondered. Emmie said you'd be right out and it was

so long I thought I'd check, to make sure you hadn't gone to sleep."

She longed to reach down and pull her robe up tight around her neck, but forced herself to give the appearance of being totally comfortable. She wouldn't let him know how much he disturbed her for anything!

"I won't be but another couple of more minutes."

"I'll wait."

He gave her a wink as he stepped back and closed the door.

Holly let her breath out in a whoosh, leaning against the wardrobe door for a second. Then, afraid he'd come back if she wasn't out in two minutes, she flew to get dressed.

The light blue dress was sleeveless, with a V-neck, fitted bodice and flared skirt. It was short, ending above her knees, but could be dressed up or down depending on the occasion. She debated for a moment, then recklessly put on her highest heels. Her feet might ache by the end of the night, but she wanted every bit of help she could muster to cope with Cache McKendrick.

Holly grabbed a light coat for later. The nights grew cold when the sun went down. She hurried to the living room. Cache stood near the window looking out.

When he heard her, he turned and watched her as she walked across the room. His face was shadowed, and a look almost of despair crossed it before the familiar teasing grin appeared.

It didn't make sense. Why would he look like that? she wondered, dismissing the idea. It must be her imagination.

Cache had no reason for despair, she wasn't that late.

"You're a very pretty lady, darlin'." His voice was low and sincere.

She smiled and inclined her head, the warmth in her heart more than she'd experienced before.

"Thank you. I don't suppose it would do any good to tell you again not to call me darling."

"Dang, I keep forgetting to call you Dr. Murphy."

Holly wrinkled her nose and shook her head. She laughed. "I give up. Just don't call me doctor in that horrid tone."

"Nobody tonight's going to believe you're a doctor, anyway. Not looking the way you do."

"What's wrong with how I look?"

"Not a dern thing, but you sure don't look like Doc Watson."

She turned away, a small bubble of happiness at his compliment.

"Let me check my latest patient and I'll be ready to go."

Cache went with her while she checked on the dog. He recognized the critter and asked her what had happened. She explained briefly as she checked the sutures. The dog was sleeping off the anesthesia. Satisfied the patient would be all right for the next few hours, she let Cache usher her out.

Another surprise awaited. Instead of the dusty pick-up truck she expected, Cache had a late model sedan, top of the line.

She hoped she hid her surprise, but wasn't sure she had when she settled on the luxurious leather seat and reached over to fasten her seat belt.

"Weren't expecting this, were you?" His teasing struck again.

"I expected your truck."

The two of them in the warmth of the car in the late afternoon sun had her imagination on overdrive. She wanted him to kiss her. The image was so clear, it was all she could do to keep herself from leaning over and touching her lips to his. She darted a quick glance as he started the engine and then looked out the windshield, holding her breath again until she could get her wayward thoughts under control.

"The truck's fine for work, but this is for play."

"Of course," she murmured.

When a couple of minutes went by and he said nothing, she turned to look at him. Startled Holly realized Cache watched her closely. Then slowly, deliberately, he shifted his gaze to skim across her lips, trace down her throat to the dark shadow showing in the V of her dress.

Holly's heart pounded in her chest. She watched as Cache's tongue darted out to lick his lips. She mimicked the movement, slowly licking her own dry lips.

His eyes caught the gesture and he stared at her moist mouth for endless moments.

Holly thought she'd scream with tension, throw herself against him and kiss him until dawn. When he looked up into her eyes, she knew he saw exactly how she felt.

"Good grief, Holly, stop looking like that or we won't make the dance." His voice was low, almost a growl.

She tried to drag her eyes away, but couldn't. She could only stare into the pools of blue that stared back at her. Lost to time and place. Lost in Cache McKendrick's blue eyes.

Four

Holly dragged her gaze from Cache's and looked down at her hands lying loosely in her lap. Her heart pounded so hard she was sure he heard it. They could probably hear it in the next county.

"It won't take long to get to the Grange Hall. That's where the dance is."

He put the car in gear and backed from her drive, glancing at her down bent head.

"Is this a special dance or are there dances all the time?" she asked, trying to fuse normality into the conversation.

She was completely self-conscious with his nearness. The suit made him seem like a businessman, but he couldn't hide that rugged cowboy air he carried without even knowing it.

"Twice a year the Grange puts on a dance, once in summer and then again at Christmas."

Holly sighed softly. Where would she be come Christmas?

"Tell me a little about yourself, darlin". I know you're not from around here, nor even California, not with that southern accent. Where are you from?"

"Kentucky," she said again homesick for the gently rolling

hills that would be green with blue grass now.

The white fences separating the pastures and paddocks of the horse farms that abounded in the area would be freshly painted. The old oaks would shade the pastures, leaves fluttering gently in the evening breeze.

Nothing in Kentucky was like the endless open sky here in California, the rolling grasslands that were already bleached by the hot summer sun, the hazy granite mountains rimming the valley in the distance. This land was big and bold. She slid a quick peek at Cache; he matched the land.

"You're a long ways from home," he commented as he passed the false fronts on the stores on Redbud's main street, light spilling out from display windows, one or two establishments still open.

"I came to California to do my vet training."

"Decided to stay?"

"No, I'm going back after this assignment."

Cache flicked a glance at her.

"For a visit, or to stay?"

"To stay. In Kentucky," Holly said firmly, hoping in her heart that it was possible.

After all this time, she still wanted to be able to build her career at Windmere as the resident vet. Surely her uncle would at least listen to her proposal. Give her a chance. Family should count!

"Doc Watson's getting old; he might consider taking on an assistant, if you do the job right."

"I wouldn't be interested. I'm going back to Kentucky."

She smiled to herself. That was an unexpected comment—

from doubting her when she first arrived to suggestion she work permanently with his favorite vet.

Cache turned into the graveled parking lot in front of the large Grange Hall. The old wooden building was painted red. A metallic roof arched over the high walls. The parking lot was crowded with cars, pick-up trucks and even a couple of horses tied near the entryway. Cache found a spot and soon escorted Holly up the shallow steps to the entrance of the old building.

Inside, the foyer was large, paneled in dark wood, with a cloakroom to the right. Cache took her coat and hung it up for her. Holly could hear the music, the murmur of voices, laughter from the main hall. She took a deep breath, ready to meet the people of Redbud.

Cache joined her in the doorway to the cloakroom, leaning over a little so that his face was close to hers. His hand caught her chin and tilted her face toward his.

"I hope you have a good time tonight. I'll introduce you to as many people as I can. But remember who brought you and who's planning to take you home," he said softly.

She looked up at him and nodded. Who else would she go off with? Was he unsure of himself? She doubted it. He was too confident, too cocky.

"I'll remember," she promised.

She wanted to laugh at the absurdity, but kept her expression serious. Though she wondered if he were teasing again.

He rubbed his thumb gently over her lips, his eyes following the movement, then caught her gaze again. Holly felt her legs began to liquefy and wondered if she sank into a puddle would he sink down with her?

"Good." His voice was low, caressing, sexy.

Two teenage girls came giggling into the cloakroom, pausing only a moment when they saw Cache and Holly.

"Hi, Cache," one said, then giggled with her friend as they slung sweaters on hangers and ran out.

"If they hadn't dashed out I could have introduced you to Bob Brunson's daughter and her friend Jasmine. They're inseparable. Both in high school," he said.

"Maybe we'll catch up with them later," she murmured, already trying to remember names.

Cache took Holly's elbow and escorted her into the large Grange Hall. It looked festive with balloons, streamers and flowers everywhere. Small tables with chairs lined the perimeter, some occupied, others vacant, each covered with a snowy white cloth, a candle burning in the center. A long row of tables along the back wall were loaded with finger food and two big bowls of punch. There was a small band in the right corner already playing for those who wanted to dance.

It was festive and pretty and Holly felt her spirits rise.

"I like this song—come on."

Cache took her hand and led her to the center, swinging Holly around and beginning to move to the music.

"Texas Two-step—you know it?" he asked as he guided her into the dance.

"I've heard of it."

She was trying to follow him, watching others, listening to the music. Holly liked all kinds of music and wondered only fleetingly if tonight's fare would be entirely country-and-western. She followed Cache's lead, tried to study the others dancing and in only a few moments felt comfortable and relaxed with the dance steps.

As soon as the music ended, they were surrounded by people wanting to meet Holly.

"This here the new vet?" an older man asked. His mustache was gray, his eyes gray, and his suit gray.

"Sure is. Holly Murphy, meet Doc Bellingham. He's the people doc," Cache said as they shook hands.

"Us doctors have to stick together, right?"

The older man smiled at Holly. When the music started he asked her to dance. With a brief nod from Cache, Holly agreed.

The evening passed quickly. She met ranchers, shopkeepers and teachers. The wives were friendly, the men as strong and rugged as Cache. Emmie came over to introduced Holly to her husband Albert and then the two chatted for the length of a dance. Everyone seemed to be having a good time.

The music segued from western to rock, then to slow, dreamy songs. Never lacking for partners, she danced almost every dance. Once or twice she caught sight of Cache—dancing with a different woman each time. Yet time and time again he caught her up and they swung in step to the music.

As the evening grew late, Holly wondered if she dared ask to sit out a dance. She was hot and thirsty and would love a cool lemonade. And, as she'd known, her feet were hurting her. She smiled at her partner at the end of the song and turned to find a chair.

"My turn again, I think."

As the music drifted into a slow, romantic song, Cache caught her around the waist and turned her to face him.

Holly's fatigue miraculously vanished. She lifted her arms to encircle his neck without a word of protest. His own arms pulled her against him as the lights in the hall dimmed slightly. Her breasts pressed against the hard muscles of his chest, her legs moved in and out between his as they danced and turned and swayed with the melody.

Cache lowered his head, resting his cheek against the top of her head. Holly closed her eyes, drifting along with the music, charmed by the man who held her in his arms. She forgot her thirst and hurt feet. She reached out to thread her fingers through the thick hair at the back of his head, wanting the moment to go on forever.

Though Cache was taller, he accommodated his steps to hers, his hands firm and caressing gently as they rested against her spine. She enjoyed being with him, dancing in a cloud of pleasure, swaying and moving to the soft romantic strains.

"Mmm, nice," Cache said softly, his fingers moving against her back. She shivered a little as she felt the heat of his fingers, his touch gentle yet inflaming.

Holly felt her defenses slip away as she enjoyed the tactile sensations Cache evoked. His hands, his chest, the strength of his body. She smiled, tonight was wonderful.

The song ended and the lights came up. Holly stepped back and stared up at Cache, blinking a little in the sudden brightness. His eyes were dark as they gazed down at her, his hands still on her back, his fingers still touching. Her own hands hadn't left his neck, and it was difficult to bring them down.

Cache's lop-sided smile lit his face and he dropped his arms, taking her elbow in one hand. "Come on, let's get something to eat and drink. The band's taking a break for a while and we'll take advantage of it."

The food tables were crowded with others with the same idea. Holly and Cache had to stand in line to get refreshments. Talking with others as they waited, Holly was slowly starting to associate faces with names.

"Cache, we came late. In fact I thought we were never going to get here. Hey." A pretty blonde girl came up to them in line and stopped beside Cache. She put her hand on his arm and left it there as she smiled prettily around at the others.

"You promised me a dance, remember?" she said with a smile, but Holly heard a slight edge to her tone. That voice was familiar.

"Sure did, sugar. Night's not over yet. Unlike you, I got here early and have worked up a thirst dancing," Cache answered easily, shifting back slightly. "I'll look for you after the band gets back."

She tossed her head, noticeably annoyed. She looked at Holly, a challenge shining from her eyes.

"And you're the new vet, I hear," the girl said, moving slightly closer to Cache.

"Holly Murphy, Sally Lambert. Sally, this is Doc Watson's locum," Cache introduced them, his eyes moving from one to the other, the teasing lights clear.

"How do you do?" Holly asked, smiling politely at the

younger girl.

If looks could kill, she'd be dead. Sally didn't want anyone around Cache, that much was evident.

"I do just fine." Sally turned back to Cache, her eyes dancing. "I heard the funniest thing earlier. You and the doc came in together and everyone was saying you brought her."

She laughed softly, inviting Cache to share the joke.

His eyes twinkled down at her and then at Holly. "They're right. I brought the doc and I'm going to be taking her home."

Holly looked at him sharply. For a moment she thought he meant to take her to his home. And keep her for always.

She met his grin and smiled back, afraid to glance at Sally Lambert, not wanting to see the look in that girl's eye.

"Well, I guess the joke's on me. I didn't think you ever brought anyone to these things."

Sally's voice was brittle, the smile plastered on, but Holly could see the sudden hurt in the girl's eyes.

"Haven't in a while. It took quite a woman to accomplish that. Right, darlin'?" Cache caught Holly's eye and taunted her.

Anger flashed again. Blast it, couldn't he see that Sally had a crush on him? Didn't he care that he was hurting her feelings?

And why wouldn't he stop calling her darling?

She longed to say something that would cut him down to size. She even opened her mouth, but nothing came out. Closing it, she looked from him to Sally.

"Actually, he brought me so I could meet people. So they'd feel comfortable calling me if they need a vet."

She tried to smooth things over. No need for drama tonight.

Sally let her hand slide from Cache's arm and nodded, that same smile plastered on her face.

"Sure. Well, see you around, Doc. Cache, I'm still counting on the dance."

"I'll find you later," he promised.

Holly didn't speak after Sally moved across the large room. She purposefully kept her eyes averted, scanning the room, studying the tables with all the food piled high. It was none of her business how Cache McKendrick ran his life, but he'd been rude to Sally. It was not what she expected of the man.

Filling her plate and getting a large glass of punch when they reached the tables, Holly followed Cache to a small table towards the back. It had seats for four, but was miraculously still empty. Only moments before she'd been elated at the thought of being alone with him. Now she wished another couple would join them to help cover the awkwardness.

She sat and took a long sip her punch.

"Okay, out with it. You think I didn't handle Sally very well, don't you?"

Cache's voice was hard as he sat beside her, putting down his plate, his food forgotten as he nailed her with his eyes. His lips were tight and a muscle twitched in his cheek.

Holly met his gaze. It was the second time he'd seemed to read her mind. She wasn't used to it. But if he wanted an honest answer, she was the one to give it to him.

"I think you were rude to her, " Holly answered. "She's

crazy about you. You could have been nicer to her."

"She's been fixated on me for ages. What am I to do, be polite and have her fancy herself in love with me all her life? She's a child. I don't want anything to do with her, except as a neighbor. I've tried being friendly, but she just thinks that means more, a lot more. So tonight I came on a little strong. Either way I lose."

He looked away, his face expressionless.

Holly stared at him suddenly seeing it from his side.

"Maybe what you did wasn't so bad. I felt sorry for her, she looked so hurt."

"It's time she grew up. I haven't brought a woman to anything like this in ages, until tonight. Maybe she'll realize I had all the time in the world to bring her if I was ever going to. I'm not. I'm not interested in Sally Lambert."

He paused for a long moment, then swung back to look at Holly.

"But I am interested in you, Holly Murphy."

Her heart raced again. He was all most women would want in a man. But she had a different goal than getting married and living in California.

"Don't be. Cache, I'm only here for a few months, then I'm leaving. I have to go back to Kentucky."

"Have to? Why? Someone there waiting for you?"

She dropped her gaze, toyed with her food and tried to find the words.

"Ever since I was a little girl, I've wanted to work at my uncle's stables. He raises and races thoroughbred horses. It's the whole reason I became a vet. I've trained, studied, gained some experience. It's been my dream for as long as I can remember. And now it's almost here. And nothing and nobody's going to get in my way."

Cache stared at her for a moment, then nodded once.

"Yeah, well, hold on to it, darlin". Dreams can shatter so easily. I hope you realize yours, Holly."

He sat back, his eyes still on her, a hint of sadness in their depths.

When Cache looked over at the people milling around, talking and laughing together, he tried to absorb some of the happiness that seemed everywhere.

He'd thought he'd finally found someone with whom he might take a chance. To see if together they could build something lasting.

Now even before he had an opportunity to explore that, she'd ended it with her quiet voice and shared dream.

A dream that never included him.

Heck, who was he kidding? He'd tried that route once. It'd ended in heartbreak and death. He was too old and too wary to try again. Second chances rarely came along. A man had to deal with the cards dealt him.

Holly didn't know what had changed, but the sparkle and delight in the evening faded. She nibbled at the food, sipped the lemonade. And watched Cache who seemed a million miles away. She was tired, confused and lonely. She glanced up as another couple joined them at the table. Her wish had been granted.

As was the way in ranching communities, the talk soon centered on cattle, horses and hay crops. The couple who joined them were Betty and Martin Basner, an older couple who lived beyond the Lone Tree ranch on the same highway. Martin and Cache discussed cattle prices and the estimated feed costs for the coming year.

Betty laughed at the men and smiled at Holly.

"Give a cattleman another one and they can talk those smelly beasts all day long."

Holly nodded with a smile. "So I see."

"There're more important things than cattle. Did Emmie give you a rundown on the stores in town? It's a good day's trip over the mountains to Reno, so we try to make sure we have as much as we want here in town."

"Emmie told me where the grocery store was and a few other shops."

"Well, when you're a hundred and eight like her, maybe shopping isn't her thing."

Holly smiled at the reference to Emmie's age. She wasn't that old.

Betty gave Holly the scoop on the various shops in town and where the best value could be found. She also included things that could only be bought in a Reno. Holly felt she could hold off until the six months were over before needing a trip to Reno.

It sounded like Betty went at least once a month.

"Do you ride?" Betty then asked.

"I used to all the time. But I haven't lately–no horse."

It was one thing Holly missed most about being away from home. She'd ridden since she was four. The best times of her teenage years had been the afternoons she had exercised her uncle's horses.

"I've got plenty. Come out some time and give them some exercise," Cache said easily, tilting back in his chair.

He ought to let her go. She'd made her position crystal clear. But he was never one to do what he ought to. If it meant he'd see her some more, even for only six months, he'd have her ride every horse on the place.

"I'd like that."

Holly smiled, suddenly pleased. She didn't realize he'd been listening. It'd be wonderful to go riding again. She looked at him, but there didn't seem to be any hidden agenda with the offer.

"I'll let the other men know you can ride whenever you show up. In case I'm not there," Cache said.

The band returned and started up immediately. Martin pulled Betty to her feet and they were out on the dance floor as if they didn't hurry they'd miss a dance. Cache looked at Holly. "Ready?"

"Yes." Her feet still hurt but they were getting numb.

"One more now and then for sure I want the last one." He swept her into his arms and led her to the dance-floor.

Holly felt awkward with the recent conversation ringing in her ears. He was interested in her and she'd told him she'd soon be leaving. Now what?

"Relax, darlin'", we both know the rules now and no one has to do anything they don't want to. Maybe we can make some beautiful memories to last down the years."

He drew her in closer and smiled down into her eyes, his hand again tracing feathery patterns against her back, holding her snug against him.

He knew all about memories to hold on to for all the years. That's all he had left of his marriage.

Now he knew the score. He wouldn't let himself get too involved with this lovely lady. She'd made it clear she wasn't for him. He knew better than to run afoul of fate by now.

"I like happy memories," she said softly, leaning against him, knowing this night would be one of the happy ones. Would he want to see her again? Make other memories?

"Happy? Or exciting?" he murmured as he dipped his head to trace feathery kisses along the side of her face, resting his cheek against her hair.

Everything connected with this man was exciting.

Holly found herself looking for Cache as the evening drew to an end. She saw him dance once with Sally, a fast-moving dance, nothing slow for that young woman. She saw him dance with Betty and with Dr. Bellingham's wife. Each time the band paused she wondered if it was to declare the final song.

All too soon it was announced. Magically Cache appeared and swept her into his arms for the last time that night. His smile was cocky and brash, just like the first day she'd seen him, but his arrogant attitude didn't rankle the way it usually did.

The lights dimmed until Holly could scarcely see. But her cowboy knew where she was. As if by long habit, her arms encircled his neck, her fingers threaded themselves into his thick hair, relishing the feel of it. Delighting in the feel of his arms around her, the solid strength of his muscular body against her softness, the feeling of anticipation and reckless danger that seemed to cling to him. He was probably the most exciting man she'd ever known.

He didn't speak. Together they moved slowly to the music. When Holly felt his lips on her cheek, then brush her mouth, the dreamy feeling intensified.

"I'm having the most marvelous evening, I never want it to end," she said so softly she could hardly hear her own voice.

"Is that an invitation for me to pay the band to keep on going?" Cache's amused voice asked softly in her ear.

Holly looked up in surprise. "You could do that?"

She stared up into his laughing face, trying to see him in the dark, furious that she'd voiced her thoughts aloud.

He twirled her around quickly twice and then leaned over and kissed her again. "Come on, let's leave now, before the crowd starts to move and we get caught in Redbud's biannual traffic jam."

He threaded his fingers through hers and led her from the dance-floor, avoiding other couples, heading for the cloakroom and the door.

In what seemed like only moments they were pulling into Holly's driveway.

"Thank you," she began primly, nervously clenching her hands beneath the draped coat.

"I'd say the pleasure's all mine, but I think you had a good time, too."

"Oh, I did. I had a wonderful time." She smiled. It'd been a great night.

"Glad you changed your mind, then?" he drawled.

She gave him a mock-frown.

"You didn't have to throw that up at me. So I was wrong to say no initially. I'm big enough to admit it. And correct the mistake."

"I'm glad you came tonight, Holly. I'll walk you to your door."

Holly watched as he rounded the front of the car. Should she invite him in? Or just say goodbye on the doorstep? What if he kissed her again? Not little brushes like at the dance. But a full bore kiss like he had at the barn.

Her heart began pounding at the thought and she shivered slightly.

"Cold?" he asked as he opened the door.

"Just a little."

He held her coat for her to thrust her arms inside and then threw his arm around her shoulders and escorted her up to the front door.

The porch light was on, as was one small lamp inside. Holly unlocked the door, still wondering whether to invite him in or not.

He turned her to face him, his arms coming round her, his face lowering to hers. His lips were warm and firm as they moved against her. His tongue teased, then boldly thrust in to the sweet moistness of her mouth.

Holly could scarcely breathe as the explosion of delight and delicious feeling cascaded through her body. His hands cradled her head as he drank from her lips. Holly gripped his wrists, holding on for dear life, reveling in the enchantment his kiss wrought. He'd offered her happy memories, or exciting ones.

If this was exciting, she picked this.

When he slowly lifted his head, Holly didn't want him to stop. She'd had one or two boyfriends along life's way, but no one like Cache.

"Come any time to the ranch. There'll always be a horse waiting," he said.

She nodded. "Thank you," she said softly.

Without another word, he turned and left.

Holly didn't move for long moments after the red tail-lights of the car disappeared down the road. Then, slowly, as if awakening from a dream, she turned and went into the house, a smile still on her lips. The lips that still yearned for more kisses from Cache McKendrick.

For a moment, Kentucky seemed a long way off.

Three days later she decided she'd waited long enough. She was caught up on work. No one needed her services. She hurried to her bedroom and pulled out her boots. Three days after the invitation to use his horses was time to show she was interested in riding, but not throwing herself after him. She'd show up and if he was there, fine. If not, he said he'd let his men know she had a standing invitation.

It wasn't as if she was going to see him. She'd made that very clear at the dance.

She'd love to ride again. It'd been several years since she'd ridden regularly, though when working at the riding academy she'd been able to snatch a ride now and then.

She told Emmie where she was going and took off. She knew the way perfectly now and before long recognized the drive to the Lone Tree Ranch.

There was no one working on the fences when she turned in. Holly drove all the way into the barn without seeing anyone. Several horses stood in the nearest corral, dozing in the sunshine. There were several pick-up trucks scattered around, but no sign of a soul.

She hadn't expected that. Surely there was someone who would hear her truck and look out to see who had arrived.

After waiting in the car for a few minutes, she climbed out and headed into the barn. If no one was around, she'd check on the mare and foal and be on her way. Next time she'd call first to let Cache know in advance that she was coming.

"Howdy, Doc." Sam was sitting in the tack-room, braiding some leather, the door open into the barn. A radio played music.

"Hi, Sam. I thought the place was deserted. Cache said I could come riding some time. Is today good?"

"Sure thing. He told us to expect you, didn't know when, though. I'll get him." He laid down the leather strips he was working on.

"Oh, there's no need. I can saddle a horse if you'll just let me know which one."

Holly was suddenly shy about seeing Cache.

Sam didn't say anything, got up and walked out into the yard. He reached in the nearest truck and blew the horn several times. In only a moment Cache came out of his house, slamming his hat on his head.

Following right behind him was Sally Lambert.

"Oh, lord, what now?" Holly murmured from the wide double barn doors.

She hadn't expected to see Cache and especially hadn't counted on running into Sally Lambert again.

"Howdy, darlin', come to go riding?"

Cache smiled at her as he drew near, his gaze skimming quickly over her, approval of the boots evident.

"If now's a good time. Hello, Sally."

"It's a good time," Cache said shortly.

"Cache, I just got here and you're going riding?" Sally asked, her angry glance turned to Holly.

"Sally, you've been here a half-hour. You said you wanted to see the foal, so go see him. Sam'll show you the way. Say hi to your dad for me. Come on, Holly, I'll get a horse for you. How well can you ride?"

Holly was almost afraid to turn her back on Sally, so strong was the girl's anger. But she answered Cache's questions and in only a few moments he'd picked Beau, a bay gelding from the corral, for her. He chose a big western saddle and effortlessly swung it on to the horse.

"Most of your riding was probably English, coming from Kentucky," he said as he tightened the cinch.

"Only till I came to California. I've ridden both kinds. I can ride anything."

He grunted and slapped the stirrups down. Before she knew it, Holly was lifted and placed in the saddle. He put her foot into the stirrup and ran his hand along her jeans to test for the right length.

It was all Holly could do to remain still when his warm palm moved up her leg, testing for the rub of the saddle, testing for fit.

"Cute foal. What did you name him?"

Sally came back to the yard, Sam a few feet behind her.

Cache paused and turned to face her, his hand still resting against the top of Holly's thigh, near her knee. She swallowed hard and looked at the horse's ears. She could feel Cache's hand like a brand. Her stomach began a strange dance, her skin grew warm and all her being focused on his hand, now gently caressing her leg, driving her wild.

"Starlight, because he was born at night out of Sunlight."

Holly squirmed slightly in the saddle and leaned over the far side to slip her boot into that stirrup, trying surreptitiously to dislodge his disturbing hand. To no avail. Sitting up, she gathered the reins, sliding from side to side in the saddle as if settling herself.

Cache looked up, met her eyes, his own brimming with amusement. Slowly he moved his hand back down, trailing fire the whole way. Holly glared at him and backed the horse a few steps.

"Right. Everything's fine. Where should I ride?"

She was glad her voice didn't come out as breathless as she felt. She saw Sally look at her again, speculation rampant in her face. Maybe she didn't do as good a job of covering up how she felt after all. She blamed Cache. Was he still trying to dodge the younger woman? And use her as a buffer?

Five

"Wait a minute and let me get my horse. I'll give you an overview of the ranch, show some landmarks so you can find your way around. Next time if no one's around you can get Beau yourself. I don't want you getting lost, though. It's a big spread."

Holly nodded and started her horse walking around, to feel his gait, and to avoid having to look at Sally while she waited. She could feel the angry girl's gaze.

"I want to come, too, Cache," Sally said, much as a child might when worried it'd miss a treat.

But Cache had already entered the barn. Sally paused only a moment and then followed him in, determination stamped on her face.

Sam moved to lean against the fence, his face grinning.

Holly threw him a glance, her own lips turning up in a smile.

"Little miss sure is hardheaded. Ain't no way Cache is interested in her. Don't know why she can't see it." He shook his head. "She's been hanging around for a long time. Maybe one day she'll realize the boss can pick and choose and he ain't choosing her."

"Which way should I go, Sam? I'll just walk the horse. Cache'll be able to catch up."

Holly glanced once at the barn, anxious to be on her way before she had to deal with Sally again. She hoped Cache wouldn't let her join them on their ride.

"Head to the right of the house; you'll see a trail that leads up that slight hill yonder. He'll catch up."

She nodded and started out. Skirting the house, she took the opportunity to study it. The walls were the same sandy color of the ground while the roof a reddish-brown tile. The windows were spacious allowing lots of light into the interior.

As she passed, she saw a green backyard, with patio and flowers beneath some old trees. It was like an oasis–inviting and pretty.

Slowly Beau walked up the slight hill, following the path as if he knew the way. Holly settled into the saddle and gave herself up to the enjoyment of the ride.

In less than five minutes Cache caught up, riding a big chestnut gelding. He rode the horse as if it had been especially invented for him. He sat straight, effortlessly guiding the large horse easily slowing as he caught up with Holly. Together they crested the hill and drew to a stop to gaze across the vast expanse before them.

"This is beautiful, Cache."

Holly smiled as she stared at the endless range land that lay in front of her. To the left, small hills gently rolled off into the distance, the bleached grass dotted here and there by the dark green of the old live oak trees. Before her the flat valley floor extended for miles, in the distance a strip of green suggested water. To the right she could glimpse the mountains, shimmering in the hot sun.

He pointed out a landmark of rocks and sage, so that she'd know how to find the ranch again. Then he led the way towards the belt of green.

"It's Ash Creek. Cuts through the land here. Gets pretty low in the fall," Cache called over his shoulder.

Holly nodded, her eyes watching him as he rode. His shoulders were broad, filling his cotton shirt, his hat pulled low on his head, shading his face from the hot afternoon sun. He appeared as comfortable on his mount as any of her cousins ever had. Somehow the long stirrups and backward slant of the western saddle made him look casual though she knew the skill he evidenced.

Cache belonged to the western lands. That cowboy was nothing like her eastern cousins.

Holly's heart began a rapid beat as she continued to watch him. He was much more interesting than the ground she was riding over. There were a million questions she wanted to ask. Was he originally from Redbud? How did he own the Lone Tree at such a young age? Had he inherited it? Bought it?

Why wasn't he married?

She looked away. She didn't need to know that. It wasn't as if she had any lasting interest in him or anyone else in Redbud. She was going home when the regular veterinarian returned.

Cache was attractive, there was no denying that. Though his teasing manner might annoy some women, she was starting to get used to it. She wondered if he took anything seriously.

Holly looked toward the swath of green as they rode closer. She could see individual trees now and a grassy area on the banks of the creek. When they got close she could see it looked more like a wide, shallow river than a creek.

He drew up on the bank. The water bubbled and skimmed over pebbles, glittering in the sunlight. It didn't look deep except where the channel curved around some old cottonwoods hurrying along its way. The air was slightly cooler in the shade of the trees and Holly was glad to stop and rest. It was hot in the direct sun.

"You should wear a hat next time. This sun's brutal," Cache said.

"You're right."

Her voice was soft, agreeable. She'd stop in at the store on her way home. This wasn't the first time she'd thought about getting a hat. It made sense.

With a lithe move he dismounted and walked to the water's edge. Pulling a blue bandanna from his back pocket, he leaned over and soaked it in the cool water. Turning, he squeezed it out and carried it to Holly.

"Here, wipe down your face, it'll cool you off. Do your neck, too. You're as red as a beet."

The bandanna was slightly dripping, and water ran down his arm as he held the soaked cloth up to her. Holly took it and touched her forehead. It felt great. She patted her face, her throat, the back of her neck, the water dripping down on her shirt, on her arms, cooling her wherever it touched.

Cache waited patiently. By the time she finished, Holly felt self-conscious. She handed him back the blue cloth with a shy smile.

"Thanks, that felt great. I'll get a hat before next time," she said.

He mounted and moved his horse slightly until he was next to her, his leg brushing against her. Holly looked at him. What now?

"See that fence in the distance?" He leaned near her, pointing out the area he referred to. Holly could feel his breath brush against her cheek as she tried to find the fence. His arm was near her shoulder, his head near to hers. If she turned her face, could she touch his?

She swallowed hard, trying to find the darn fence. Her skin quivered in anticipation and longing for him to touch her. Memory of the dance flooded her and the kisses that ended the evening. Her eyes focused on his hand pointing out the fence and not the fence in the distance.

"That marks the start of the northern pastures. I run Herefords there, several hundred head. Then swing around—" His arm swept around and when Holly turned to follow it she realized his arm was almost touching her. She took a deep breath and forced herself to look where he was pointing. Focus!

"There starts the southern pastures and I run a few dozen Texas longhorns there."

"Are they doing all right here?" Curiosity took over.

"Yep, have to watch the calves a little in the winter months, but more for predators than for weather. So far they're flourishing. The Herefords are easier to deal with. But

I'm building a longhorn herd, too."

"Diversity's good," she murmured, looking back at the cool water of the river.

Did he ever come swimming here? The banks beneath the cottonwoods were grassy, green and inviting. The water shallow, but better to just sit in it and let the coolness flow over her. Maybe she'd bring her swimsuit some time when she came to ride.

"Plus the longhorns have leaner meat. That's the trend today, so I want to follow the market."

They ambled along the river for a couple of miles, talking casually about ranching, cattle and horses. It was comfortable in the dappled shade by the water.

Holly longed to ask him other questions, personal ones, to learn more about him, but fear of his mocking tongue kept her quiet.

He was too much on her mind, she decided. In the future, she'd try to come riding when he wasn't around. Though the rides would not be as much fun, a small voice whispered inside her.

When they returned to the stables, no one else was in sight. Cache dismounted and threw the reins over the top bar of the fence. Holly slid off Beau and threw his reins over his head, holding them in one hand.

"I'll help you put the horses away," she said.

"Come on, I'll show you where Beau paraphernalia's kept. He doesn't work as much as he once did so you can ride any time," Cache said, starting for the barn.

Holly nodded and followed. It took only a short time to

unsaddle and brush down the horses. That Holly knew how to do. How many hours had she groomed the horses in her uncle's stables? She loved the warmth of the animals, the routine of long strokes along the back and sides. She picked Beau's hooves and then gave him a final pat when she was finished.

"He goes in the first stall. It's late enough he can eat now. I'll turn him out into the corral later," Cache said, finished with his horse. He put Roman into a stall two down from Beau.

Holly walked the horse in and patted him again. Leaving, she latched the half door securely. "No hay in the trough," she said.

"One of the men can see to it," Cache said.

"I don't mind helping. Is it up there?" She pointed to the loft.

"No. There some bales in the back beyond Sunlight's stall."

Holly followed when Cache walked back, stopping to talk to Sunlight and admire the colt as it jumped around in the large stall.

"Looks like mama could use some hay, too," she commented, rubbing the velvety nose.

"I'll fill them all up while I'm at it," Cache said.

Holly spotted the bale of hay that had been cut open, flakes already broken apart. Cache picked up several and started down one side of the barn, tossing flakes into the troughs of each stall. Most were empty, the horses still out working.

She put a flake in Beau's feeder and one in the new

mother's. She stopped to pet the colt who came to the door his curiosity strong.

As she walked back to the hay to get another load, Cache was right behind her.

It was hot in the barn from the heat of the sun beating on the roof. The sweet smell of hay permeated the air. Holly wished she had Cache's wet, cool bandanna again. A faint sheen of perspiration coated her brow. She was hot all over. When she got home, she'd take a cool shower first thing!

"It's hot," he said, wiping an arm against his forehead and taking a step closer to Holly.

Involuntarily, she stepped back. Away from the dizzy feelings she got whenever Cache came too close.

"Take off your shirt, if you're hot," she said, looking for the bandana. Did he still have it?

"I will if you do." Cache's voice was low, teasing, his eyes dancing with laughter. He took a step forward.

Holly blinked at the blatant invitation. She shook her head and grinned.

"No thanks. I'll head for home and a quick shower."

He stepped closer, his eyes holding hers. She stepped back, he stepped forward. She stepped again, came up against the pile of stacked bales of hay. He followed until he almost touched her. His eyes never left hers, but the laughter faded, to be replaced by something intense and hot.

Holly's breath caught. She couldn't look away. Her heart pounded. Licking suddenly dry lips, she tried to draw a breath.

Cache took off his hat and reached around Holly to put it on the stacked-up bales. He ran his other hand through his hair, darkened slightly by perspiration.

Daringly, Holly reached up one hand and ran her fingers through his hair. Cache closed his eyes at her touch, standing so near her she could feel the radiant heat from his body.

He opened his eyes and looked at her for another long moment, then lowered his head to kiss her. His lips were hot and moist moving against hers, building a response that flared in Holly like a white-hot fire.

The air was hot, his mouth was hot, the feel of him against her was hot. She thought she'd be consumed by the heat. The hay prickled against her back, through the thin cotton of her shirt as Cache leaned into her and crowded her back into the bales. Her hands encircled his neck and pulled him to her as his body pressed against hers, inflaming her further.

Unexpected delight spread through every cell. She couldn't get enough of this man. The kiss deepened–went on and on. She pressed herself against him, opening her mouth to his, giving as good as she got.

Pulling back only slightly, Cache looked down at her smoldering gaze. He smiled slightly and moved back enough to make some space between them.

"You're so beautiful," Cache said against her mouth as he again claimed her lips.

She hugged him closer.

When he moved from her mouth to trail short, sweet, hot kisses along her cheeks to her jaw, she sighed in pleasure. Then he moved lower to trace her throat with his hot.

Holly was instantly flooded with erotic fantasies as never before.

Cache sank down, pulling Holly with him. He leaned back until he was sitting on the hard wooden floor, the pricks of the hay unnoticed against his back as he brought her to sit in his lap.

Holly reached for his mouth, the pleasure and delight he was bringing beyond anything she'd ever experienced before. It was heady, indecent and oh, so exciting.

He'd been right–exciting memories were far better to make than sweet ones.

Holly didn't know which was better—to receive his kisses or give back some measure of her delight when kissing him. She was so hot and her mouth felt swollen with passion. Her fingers tingled with the feel of every inch of his body she could reach–his strong muscles, his arms, his neck; the thickness of his hair, the roughness of his cheeks, the hardness of his jaw.

"Cache? You in here boss?"

Instantly they froze.

For a long moment Holly didn't move a muscle, except for her pounding heart and her ragged breathing. She couldn't move. Slowly she pulled back a little, staring in shocked surprise at Cache. She looked over her shoulder. They had rounded the corner of the wall. No one could see them–yet.

"Boss? You in here?"

It was Sam, somewhere at the other end of the barn. But from the sound of things, he was walking their way.

Cache sprang up. He looked for his hat, reached for it as he stepped out in to the main aisle of the barn.

"Yeah, Sam. What's up?"

In an embarrassed panic, Holly brushed the hay off the

best she could. Holding her breath, she leaned against the wall separating her from the main part of the barn.

"You have a call from Miz Eton. She says it's important and I should find you. She's holding," Sam said.

"Okay. I don't know what's so important, but I'll take the call."

Holly stood stock still listening as Cache and Sam walked back to the front of the barn. When she no longer heard them, she peeked around the edge of the wall. Sunlight had her head over the half door, watching Holly.

Otherwise the barn was deserted.

Her heart still raced, but her breathing was under control. Quickly she walked out of the barn and to her truck. She glanced at the house but didn't see anyone. And she wasn't going to wait.

Starting the truck, she backed it around and headed for home. Glancing at herself in the rear-view mirror she saw that her lips were rosy and swollen from his kisses. There was hay in her hair and she reached up to pick it out.

"Stupid!"

She hit the steering wheel in frustration and embarrassment. She was supposed to be in Redbud in a professional capacity, not to become involved with one of the local cowboys, no matter how sexy.

Her plans were made. Set in concrete. It'd been her dream for seven long years. The dream had been even longer, if she counted all the time as a child she'd yearned to be the vet at Windmere.

She wouldn't let a few passionate kisses change all that.

Hot and sticky by the time she reached home, she hurried inside, glad Emmie had left for the day. She dashed into the bathroom and took a long cool shower.

She stood beneath the water, enjoying it as it cascaded over her body. Washing her hair, she gave a brief prayer that all the animals around town would stay well for the foreseeable future. She hoped she didn't have to go out anywhere else today. She wanted to dress in shorts and a sleeveless top and sit around and do nothing the rest of the day.

When she was dressed, she wandered back to the office. The flashing light told her there were messages on her machine. For a moment she felt guilty. She should have listened before her shower. What if there was an emergency?

She had her pager with her. Emmie would have found her if there had been an emergency.

Pressing the button, she sat on the edge of the desk to listen. Emmie called to remind her she'd be coming late in the morning. Dr. Bellingham called to invite her to dinner in two days. Mike Slatter called to ask the doc to arrange some time to come and check on his bull, he seemed listless.

Probably because of the heat, Holly thought.

The last voice was Cache's.

"Darlin'", forgot to ask if you can go with us when we check on the calves before weaning. You can give them their inoculations. We'll be gone a few days up to the summer pastures. Stan over at Overvilla usually subs for Doc Watson when Doc comes with us. If you can't go, I'll get Stan and you can sub for him. Call me."

Her heart beat against her ribs as she listened to the

familiar voice.

She knew why he had forgotten to mention the trip.

Dared she go? For a moment she let her imagination run riot, then reined it in. It wouldn't be the two of them. There'd be cowboys around, horses, cattle. There was work to do.

She called Dr. Bellingham to accept the dinner invitation. She then called Mike Slatter to set up an appointment in the morning to examine his prize bull.

She looked up the number and called Stan Connors to see if he could sub.

Lastly she called Cache to agree to the cattle trip.

"We'll leave next Wednesday. Shouldn't be gone more than four or five days. You want me to call Stan?" He was all business.

"I've already called Stan. I need to call him back to give him the exact days. What do I bring?"

"Just medical supplies. We'll have everything else. Oh and your clothes. It gets cold at night, so bring something warm. Thanks, Doc."

Before she could even ask if he was talking about the Herefords or longhorns, he hung up. Holly stared at the phone for a long moment, then slowly replaced it.

She'd have a reason to talk to him next time she went riding–to find out more about this cattle trip. How many vials of vaccines to bring. And exactly what was expected of her.

Holly stayed away from the Long Tree for three days.

That seems to be my limit, she thought as she turned into the driveway in the early afternoon of the third day. She'd brought a cowboy hat and had on a clean shirt and jeans. Her hair was pulled neatly back in a braid.

The yard was as deserted as before when she drove up. She grabbed her hat and walked into the dim light in the barn. Pausing a moment to let her eyes adjust after the bright sun, she checked on Sunlight and Starlight before going to get Beau, dozing in his stall. She called his name softly as she walked up to his door, so as not to startle him.

He came awake and turned to thrust his muzzle against her open hand. Holly stroked him for a few minutes, the soft, velvety feel always a pleasure. She patted his neck and reached for the halter hanging on a hook by the door, talking to him the entire time.

"Want to go for a ride, old fellow?" she crooned.

One more quick glance around showed her she was still alone. She cross-tied him and found the saddle she'd used before. In only minutes she and the gelding were heading past the ranch house and out to the open pasture beyond.

Some distance from the house she urged to horse to a lope and they thundered across the range towards the river, the hot air streaming by, giving a momentary illusion of coolness. When they drew near the water, she turned towards the south, pulling Beau into a jog-trot and then finally into a walk.

"I don't want you getting too hot," she said as she patted his damp neck. There were plenty of things to see and Holly didn't want to miss anything.

After an hour, she moved towards the landmark Cache had shown her before. They slowly picked their way through some rocks, the horse surefooted and steady on the uneven ground. Holly was hot and sweaty now and feeling wilted. The hat kept her shaded from the sun, but she was still in direct sunlight and wished for some sort of breeze.

Near the top of the rise, she saw a small black ball of fur struggling near some rocks. She drew in the horse and studied the situation. It appeared that the small animal's paw was trapped by a cleft in a rock. It struggled, whining softly. Resting only a moment, it frantically tried pulling its paw free. It was not happening.

Holly couldn't ignore an animal in distress, though she saw with a shock the white stripe down its back.

"Well, now what?" she said aloud. The horse's ears twitched, but he stood patiently, awaiting her signal to proceed. The little skunk mewed softly, scrambling against the rocks, trying to dislodge his paw. But he was tightly trapped.

"Blast it all," Holly said as she dismounted.

Six

Holly reined in near the house, looking at the men in the yard near the barn. It looked as if every cowboy on the blasted ranch was standing around. She thought about her arrival earlier when she didn't see soul. Why not this time?

She saw Cache leaning casually against her truck, talking to one of the younger men.

Three others were in the corral, lethargically lassoing the horses, releasing them. Just for practice, as far as she could tell. Two more were leaning against the rail fence, watching the ropers.

"Well dern," she said again under her breath, breathing through her mouth, knowing there was no avoiding them.

She just wanted to get home and wash and get rid of the smell of skunk.

But she hated to have to announce it to the world.

Maybe she'd bypass the house, ride down the drive to the main road and ride Beau home, coming back after she'd showered.

Too late. Someone must have seen her and told Cache. He turned and looked in her direction, pushed off from the truck and started walking towards her.

Holly bit her lip in indecision, watching him approach her, his step easy, his body moving with the smooth fluid motion of a wolf on the prowl. She shivered slightly as she watched him approach, feeling pinned by his gaze. She wished she could turn around and ride away. Outride the stench.

Instead, she urged the horse forward slowly, moving as if in a trance towards the man. It was inevitable, might as well get it over with.

Cache stopped a few feet from her and she pulled Beau to a stop. The horse had performed perfectly, despite the stench.

"Whew, is that you?" he said, his face frowning at the stench that filled the air.

She tilted her chin slightly and nodded crisply. "I found a skunk caught in some rocks. I had to help him."

"You're lucky Beau brought you home."

The corners of his mouth twitched as he reached out to grab the rein near the horse's mouth.

"Once we started going, I was downwind of him."

She dismounted, jumping a little the last few inches. She was not tall enough on this slope to reach the ground with a foot in the stirrup.

She eyed him warily. "You want to bring my truck here for me and I won't have to share this with all your men?"

Cache grinned, shook his head. "You don't want to be doing that, darlin'. You'll never get the smell out of the truck. I'll take old Beau here back to the barn. One of the men can take care of him. You need a bath."

"I'll get one at home."

"And have skunk fragrance be your companion the rest of the summer?"

She frowned. She didn't want her truck to smell like skunk. She was almost sick from it herself right now. She only wanted to wash it all off and never have to smell it again.

Cache made sense.

"Okay," she agreed reluctantly.

"Did you help him?" he asked as he led the horse toward one of the other cowboys.

Holly stayed several feet away–as if that would help.

"That was the only thing that went right. He was trapped in some rocks. I managed to him free. Fine thanks he gave me."

She laughed a little. She'd known he'd probably spray her, but she couldn't let him stay trapped.

"Where did he get you?"

"All over, can't you tell?"

"Boots?"

"Maybe not. I hope not." She looked at the boots, dusty and dry. How could she tell? She thought the spray had hit her as she was turning away, trying to evade the little critter's shot.

"Definitely on my shoulder and hair. Yuck, I've felt sick ever since."

"Wait here."

He led Beau across the space and spoke briefly with one of the cowboys. In only a moment, Holly could hear the laughter as the tale spread. She saw the men turn to look her way.

"Wait until you have an embarrassing moment," she

muttered beneath her breath as Cache started back towards her.

All sorts of scenarios flashed in her mind for getting even with him. But, she sighed, none would probably come true.

When he got near her, he veered around, motioning for her to follow him. Holly couldn't really blame him. She did smell awful. And she didn't want to get the stench on anything else.

Around to the back of the house then he stopped and looked at her.

"I'll help you get your boots off. No sense in getting them messed up if you don't need to."

She eyed him suspiciously. "What do you mean?"

He smiled. "Now, darlin', how do you get rid of skunk stink?"

"Hose it off."

"Nope, that won't do it."

"With soap?"

He shook his head. "Not plain soap. I've got just what you need inside. You aren't the only one to get sprayed around here. Wait here."

He entered the house, leaving Holly standing in the dusty yard. She couldn't see the barn or any of the corrals from where she stood. All she could see were the hills and the endless blue sky. And smell of skunk.

Cache appeared with a large bucket, dish washing soap and a bottle of hydrogen peroxide and a washcloth.

She watched as he filled the bucket with the hydrogen peroxide, added the liquid soap and then a small amount of baking soda. The concoction began to fizz.

"Sit down so we can get your boots off," he said, a pained expression on his face.

Holly didn't blame him, she reeked.

He waited until she sat on the steps, then put down the bucket and cloth and reached to pull off her boots. He sniffed them before placing them near the door. "They don't smell, at least I don't think so. You're doing a good job of polluting the air."

"I couldn't leave it there without helping it," she said.

"This'll cut through the skunk oil. It's the only thing I know that cuts it clear through. Then you can hose it off. Otherwise the smell could linger for days."

"I can't imagine. I just want to stop the smell before I puke."

"Strip off your clothes."

"What did you say?" She looked at him in shock.

His eyes dancing; he pushed his hat back on his head.

"Take off your clothes. They probably got the worst of the spray. I'll find something for you to wear home. These should be burned. You'll never get rid of the stink."

"I am not going to strip down for you or anyone–" she began hotly.

He laughed.

"Darlin'", you'll never be safer. You stink to high heaven right now. You're as safe as you'll ever be."

Holly didn't like him laughing at her, but as she stared back at him she realized the truth of what he said. Not that she liked it.

And she would not strip down in front of him!

"I can do this myself. I'll pour the mixture on me in the tub."

"I don't want my bathroom smelling like this for the next two months. Wash off with this, once the worst is over, you can shower the rest off."

He stood beside her offering the bucket and cloth.

"Then I can manage by myself. Leave it and go away," she said.

"How are you going to get your back? Your hair? Come on, darlin'", stop arguing and get going. You smell awful."

"Don't keep saying that!" she snapped, unbuttoning her.

She wished she'd worn a serviceable cotton exercise bra, instead of the frilly bit of lace and cotton she had on. But he was right. She sure couldn't be called alluring . She wrinkled her nose. She did smell awful.

At least her briefs were of serviceable cotton. She stepped out of her jeans and pulled off her crew socks. Actually her bikini revealed more than today's underwear.

But telling herself that didn't help. She still felt more exposed than every before.

Cache watched her, his eyes twinkling.

"I wear cotton briefs too," he said softly, and leaned over to touch her lips lightly with his.

Holly licked her lips when he pulled back. He either really wanted to kiss her or his nose had died.

"I could throw my arms around you and give you a kiss you'd never forget," she said with a show of bravado. "Then I could share some of this delightful fragrance with you."

"Then I'd have to share your shower with you," he said, his voice low and seductive.

Holly stared into his eyes, seeing the growing awareness and hunger. Knowing it was probably reflected in her own. She swallowed and looked away, but the hunger didn't fade.

"Pour on that concoction," she said, looking firmly into the distance.

Cache's touch was impersonal as he covered her with fizzing solution, making sure to work it into her hair, along her side and back until all traces of the awful smell were neutralized.

Holly practiced thinking of other things as the cool, thick liquid dribbled over her. When she was coated to his satisfaction, he stepped back and tilted his head studying her.

She turned around facing him, raising a fist in mock-threat.

"If you say one single word, I'll deck you," she said, her eyes sparking fire.

But thankfully the smell had faded.

"I wouldn't dare," he murmured and reached for the hose.

"Oh no you don't…"

She tried to move out of the way but the blast of cold water caught her right in the face.

"It's freezing," she shrieked, dashing to one side, trying to get away.

"Hold still." He clamped one hand on her arm, dousing her with the cold water. "You can't rinse this off in the shower."

She grabbed the hose and turned it on him, smiling

gleefully at his shout of surprise.

"Maybe not, but at least you can know how cold it is."

She danced away, out of reach. Skimming the water off her, she wrung out her hair.

"I'm detoxed enough. Where's the shower?" She needed privacy.

And Cache's gaze was roving all over her. Her skin tingled as if he were caressing her with his hands, not just his eyes. She stood transfixed, watching him look at her.

"Stop that! Where's your bathroom?" she asked again, shivering a little in the hot afternoon sun.

She licked suddenly dry lips and took a step closer to the back door. She needed to get away from him, away from the thoughts that were spinning in her mind now that she could think.

His gaze narrowed and pierced hers. He started towards her, never looking away. Walking slowly with a hunter's prowl.

Holly broke eye contact and scurried across the few feet of dirt to the back door, throwing it open to enter his kitchen. She paused for a moment, not knowing which way to go.

"This way."

His voice was calm, expressionless. He led the way down a hall, entering a large bedroom at the back of the house. "Through there." He pointed out the adjoining bathroom.

Holly hurried into the room, closed the door and in only seconds was in the shower, relishing the hot water sluicing over her, quickly soaping up to get the remaining smell of dish detergent and skunk off her. She washed her hair with Cache's shampoo, its spicy tang reminding her of him. Of the night of the dance and the afternoon in the barn.

Annoyed at where her thoughts were going, she stayed beneath the spray until the water turned cool.

She dried off quickly, wrapping her hair in one towel and wrapping her body in another one. She glanced at the sodden underwear on the floor and wrinkled her nose. She didn't ever want to touch any of it. But what was she going to wear home? She couldn't drive home through town wearing only a towel.

"Doc?" Cache called through the door.

"What?"

"I've left a couple of things for you on the bed. I know they'll be large on you, but you should manage to keep them on until you get home. I'll be in the living room, back down the hall and to your right. There's also a plastic trash bag, put your clothes in it."

She heard the bedroom door close and slowly she opened the connecting door from the bath to peek out. His room was empty.

The large king-size bed dominated the space, windows flank it framing the view of the back of the house off to the horizon. Carpet on the floor muffled her steps. She saw the cut-offs and the blue cotton shirt laid out. Glancing once at the closed door, she quickly pulled up the shorts. They were a loose on her, but wouldn't fall off. She pulled on the shirt. Knowing it was his gave her a funny feeling in the pit of her stomach.

It was huge. Patiently she rolled back the sleeves until her hands were clear. She buttoned it up to the neck. If she only had a belt, she could wear it as a dress.

Cache had left a large plastic bag as well which she took into the bathroom and scooped up the sodden underwear. She tidied the bathroom, using one of his combs to attack the tangles in her hair. Finally feeling refreshed and halfway decent, she went to find her host.

He stood by the window overlooking the front yard. This room was large, airy and comfortable. It looked lived-in. Holly glanced around, discovering what she else could discern about Cache by studying how he lived.

The tan and golds of the room reflected the outdoors. The comfortable furniture showed her a man who liked comfort above fashion. Pictures on the walls were primarily outdoor western themes. Several books were scattered around, a couple of magazines on the table. She couldn't read the titles, but the cattle on the cover gave her a clue to the material inside.

He heard her and turned. "Better?"

"Much. Thanks."

She wanted to go home, put distance between herself and Cache, between herself and what happened every time the two of them were together. Yet part of her wanted to stay, spend some more time with this unsettling man.

"I brought your truck up and put your boots in." Cache moved slowly across the room, his eyes never leaving hers. "Your hat's toast, though."

Holly took a deep breath. "Thanks, I'll be going, then. I appreciate not having skunk smell in the truck. It might never come out."

"Glad to help. Next time find another way to help."

She smiled and shrugged.

"Come again and we'll go riding together."

He stopped near her, but didn't touch her.

Holly wished he would.

"Okay. I'll bring your clothes back tomorrow."

"I'll burn yours."

She nodded, with only a twinge of regret for the new shirt and new hat.

"You look like a little girl, playing dress-up," he said, his eyes drifting down over the straight hair hanging down her back, the loose shirt enveloping her, the shorts that hung to her knees.

"It's better than going home in nothing," she retorted.

"It'd be better to stay in nothing." His voice was low, husky, his eyes met hers again and she could read the invitation, loud and clear.

"I'm going back to Kentucky," she said desperately, as if that were a mantra that could protect her.

Protect her from her feelings, which threatened to get out of control around this man.

"But not today, nor tomorrow. We'd have time before you go."

His voice was soft, seductive, tempting.

"I don't think so."

She backed towards the door. She wasn't one for one-night stands. If she fell in love, she'd want constancy, permanence, marriage.

She was pretty sure those traits weren't high on Cache's list.

"Memories for the future." His voice was enticing.

"No!"

Holly whirled and hurried out of the door, the screen slamming behind her. Running from him, running from her own desire to give in to his suggestions and stay.

She lightly stepped across the short distance to her truck, her bare feet scarcely feeling the rocks and dirt, her heart thumping in her chest. Starting her truck, she pulled away, the desire to stay so strong it was almost overwhelming.

She glanced in the rear-view mirror and saw Cache standing in the doorway. For a moment she faltered, then with determination looked forward and carefully drove home.

She didn't have time to get involved with some sexy cowboy whose eyes melted her insides, whose touch inflamed her senses and whose presence filled her with delight.

He was wild and carefree and not for the likes of her. Let him chase after the girls in town, and leave her alone. Holly put temptation behind her as the ranch was left behind.

She reached home without incident. Taking another quick shower, she felt more herself with her own shampoo and clothes. The afternoon remained warm and the heat would linger far into the night. It was muggy and still and Holly wished that the house she was staying in had air-conditioning.

Sitting near a window, for what little breeze might stir, she picked up a book and began to read. The stillness was oppressive and she had no energy. Slowly she let her eyelids close and dozed off.

The shrill ring of the phone startled her awake. Holly blinked slowly and looked around, for a moment disorientated to where she was. It was almost dusk; she'd been asleep for a couple of hours. The phone on the desk in the office rang again and she dashed in to answer it.

"Hello?"

"Doc? It's Sam. Sunlight's in a bad way. She took a fall. Broke her leg. I don't know if anything can be done. Can you come to see her?"

"What is it? What's wrong?"

She'd seen the mare when she'd first arrived at the ranch that afternoon. She and her foal had been doing fine. What happened since then? She heard the shrill cries of a horse in distress.

Already Holly was thinking of what she needed to get, how long it would take her to get back to the Lone Tree ranch.

"She's down, Doc. Leg broken, maybe shattered. She's bad, Doc."

"I'll be there as fast as I can get there."

Holly slammed down the receiver and raced to grab her bag and a handful of antibiotics. She thrust her feet into tennis shoes and hurried out to the truck.

Surprised she wasn't stopped for reckless driving or speeding, in only a few minutes Holly turned into the long driveway leading to the ranch, dust spurting high behind her wheels as she sped up the road.

The sun was sinking beneath the mountains in the far distance and the last faint blue of the sky was gradually changing to darkness. She floored the accelerator and tore up the drive.

Slamming to a stop by the barn, she thrust open the door

and hurried out.

Several cowhands were by the fence, watching inside the corral. Holly looked beyond them to see the horse lying down, the two men beside her. She ran to the fence and squeezed through the rails, her bag banging against the lower one.

Sam stood beside Cache, both looking at the little mare. For a stunned moment Holly registered the gun in Cache's hand. She refused to accept what she was seeing, then reality hit her.

"No!"

She ran across the soft dirt, slowing as she drew near. The horse was on her side, her front leg twisted and mangled. She lay completely still. At first Holly didn't see the small, dark, bloody hole in the center of her forehead.

"No!" she said again almost as a groan.

Cache turned to stare at her, his face stricken, his eyes dark and anguished.

"Why didn't you wait? I might have saved her."

Holly flung herself down beside the horse, ran her experienced hands over her shoulder, down the leg that was twisted. Warmth met her fingers as she smeared blood. A jagged edge of bone protruded.

Tears streamed down her face. "Why didn't you wait?" she asked, feeling for a pulse, knowing there was not one.

"She was always a good horse. I couldn't let her suffer. You couldn't have saved her." Cache's voice was dull, his eyes almost dead.

He stared at the mare, not even looking at Holly. His hand pat her cheek, rubbed down over and over as if in comfort.

"You were a good horse, Sunlight. Always a good horse."

She stood up in front of him, ignoring Sam who started to say something, anger flashing through her. She faced Cache, frustrated with the entire situation and feeling so helpless.

Blast it all, I'm a vet! I should have been allowed to try. I might have saved her. I know what I'm doing, and there are lots of methods now that weren't available just a few years ago. You should have given me a chance! There was no need to kill her. That's not much better than murder!"

Cache swung his gaze from the horse to Holly, but didn't really see her. "Her leg was too badly broken. It couldn't have been fixed. I think she had internal injuries as well. She was in pain and couldn't get better."

"You don't know that!"

Holly was almost yelling at him. Tears continued to pour down her face as she stared at him accusingly. The ache in her chest was so strong she longed to hit him to vent some of her pain.

"You should have waited. I would have told you if there was nothing to be done. But no, you couldn't wait. The law of the old macho west, put the horse out of its misery. Don't wait for some woman who might be able to help."

His gaze gradually focused on her and he stared at her in growing horror.

"Do you really think that's what this is about? Do you think I wanted to kill her? Sunlight? Because of some macho notion of how to be a cowboy?"

"No, she doesn't think that, boss. Go on now, nothing more to be done here," Sam said softly, gently reaching out to pull the gun from Cache's unresisting fingers.

Holly turned to look at the mare, her vision blurred by the tears. She wiped her face and stood still, trying to ease the ache in her heart. Her thoughts churned.

Could she have save the horse?

What of her foal? What would the little baby do without his mother?

Tears started again. She hated to lose an animal, any animal, but most especially horses. She hated even more that she hadn't been given the chance to save it.

Cache stood and reached out to grab her shoulders, shaking her lightly.

"It was best for Sunlight, Holly."

"How do you know that?"

Wrenching away from him, she moved nearer the horse. Holly took a deep breath. She heard Cache move across the corral, the soft murmur of the men by the fence as he opened the gate and left.

"Now, Doc, you have no call to yell at Cache. He didn't want to put down Sunlight. But she was in a bad way. You weren't here, we were. She was in pain and you couldn't have fixed her. I thought maybe you could, but once we saw how bad she was I knew. We're stockmen. We know animals, too, Doc."

"Macho, chauvinistic male," she muttered, her eyes filling with tears again.

"Not so, Doc. That's probably the hardest thing he's ever done. He loved that horse. It has been a favorite of his ever since she came to the ranch. She was Trish's horse."

As if that explained it all.

Holly turned to look at him, tears still shimmering on her lashes. "Who's Trish?" She'd heard that name before.

"Cache's wife."

She turned to stare down at the dead mare. Cache's wife?

She'd heard the name several times, but never knew he was married. For a moment she remembered the big bed in the bedroom, too big for a single man.

The pain in her chest tightened a little more.

The last of the day's light had gone. As the darkness blanketed the land, Holly could scarcely see the horse any more. She turned and trudged back to the fence, opening the gate and slipped through. Without a word to anyone, she climbed into her truck and slowly started for home. The ache in her heart was for the horse and for herself.

It was still and hot when Holly parked in her driveway. She didn't go inside. Instead she sat out on the porch, on the long wooden swing that Dr. Watson had there. She knew she'd overreacted, but that mare was her first patient in Redbud. She was so proud of the new mama and her baby.

Sam was right. He and Cache and the cowboys on the ranch were stockmen. They knew horses as well as she did.

Slowly the ache in her chest began to ease. Tomorrow she'd find out exactly what happened. Determine if there would have been any chance however slim to save the mare. Tomorrow she'd handle all that. For now, she just wanted to sit and sway with the swing and not think.

The phone rang twice. Holly remained swinging, ignoring the summons. The answering machine clicked on and recorded a message, but she couldn't hear it from the porch. The pager remained silent. The calls weren't emergencies.

Slowly Holly moved to and fro in the soft, hot night.

She loved horses. She'd do anything to help them. There were so many new techniques these days to help a broken bone. It wasn't automatically a death sentence like in generations past.

She was angry. And frustrated. And sad.

She heard the vehicle before she saw the lights. The twin beams slashed through the darkness, the throaty growl filled the silence of the night. She watched as he slowed for her drive and turned in, the arc of the bright light sweeping her yard, briefly illuminating her on the porch before he cut the motor off. She sat still, watching as he opened the door.

Cache climbed out of his truck and walked up the path to the porch, pausing as he watched her warily then moved to sit gingerly beside her.

"I'm sorry," she said, before he spoke, her voice tight with tension and unshed tears.

It hadn't been fair of her to attack him. She knew that. She'd let her emotions overrule her head.

He sighed softly and pushed back so that the swing started moving.

"I didn't want to put her down, Holly. But she was suffering and there was nothing you could have done."

She nodded, then realized he probably couldn't see her.

"I just wanted to try." She was silent for a few moments, then turned to try to see him in the faint starlight. "Why are you here?"

"You were upset. I tried to reach you by phone, but you didn't answer. I wanted to make sure you were all right."

"Why?"

She'd been offensive, attacking him when he was already down. Rudely accusing him on his own turf. Why come to check on her?

"I don't know. Maybe because there was so much sadness. I didn't want you to feel bad tonight."

"Where's Trish?"

Holly bit her lip. She hadn't known she was going to ask that. She wished she'd turned on the porch light so that she could see him, see how he took her question.

"Trish died a long time ago, Holly. Sunlight was a present from me to her before she died. The mare was all I had left of a happy time."

Holly sat still, assimilating the news. She could relate. She remembered the pony her parents had given her before their death. She'd cherished that gift from them long beyond the time she'd still ridden him.

Holly reached out and found his hand, lacing her fingers through them. She didn't have words to convey her feelings. She hoped he knew from her touch.

For long silent moments, they moved back and forth on the swing.

He was hurt, vulnerable, sad. She wished she could do something to make things better.

"Do you want to tell me what happened?" she asked softly, afraid to shatter the tenuous peace.

"With Sunlight or Trish?" he asked, his voice quiet, none

of the teasing she was used to hearing. Just a great weariness.

"Either."

Suddenly Holly wanted desperately to learn about Trish. How Cache had loved her, how she'd died, how long ago. Would he ever love anyone again?

"We let Sunlight out in the corral, without Starlight, so she could run and have some sunshine. We'd already brought in some of the range horses, in preparation for the cattle trip next week. She was running tossing her head. She looked like she was having a great time. The next we looked, she was down and screaming. I don't know if she snapped the bone and then tried to run on it, or was kicked by one of the other horses. The bone was shattered. And there was swelling in her belly. I hated to put her down. She was a good horse. And she was Trish's."

She swallowed hard, aware of his pain, her own disappointment at the loss of the horse diminished in light of his own pain. She leaned against him as if her warmth could somehow heal him. Time seemed to stand still.

"I overreacted when I saw her. I'm sorry I yelled at you," she said, her fingers still threaded through his.

"Darlin'", if you react like that at every animal's death, you'll burn yourself up in no time." His voice was gentle.

"I know. That's the hardest part about this job. Animals are so helpless. They can't tell you what's wrong. I have to guess and hope I'm right every time."

"Experience helps," he said.

She nodded. "So I hear."

She began to relax with the soft rhythm of the swing,

feeling safe, secure and gradually at peace.

Time seemed to roll on slowly. Evening stars shone from the dark sky.

"Holly…"

She turned to face him and he leaned over and kissed her. His lips were warm. In only seconds the warmth penetrated her body, his mouth moving against hers and she responded.

She turned slightly to get closer and Cache pulled her into his lap. His arms went around her and he pulled her snug against him as he continued the kiss.

Holly grew warmer, breathless, consumed by feelings Cache ignited in her. Sadness turned to passion. Grief turned to yearning. Death forgotten as life-affirming emotions sparked. Her fingers traced the strong muscles of his shoulders, the taut column of his neck, his thick hair.

Sensations mingled and imprinted themselves on Holly's mind. She was lost in a world of sensuous feeling and tactile delight.

Forgotten for the moment was the sadness.

His hands were magic, his mouth enchanting, his spell catching her fast and binding her to him forever.

The low murmur of the car was lost in the pounding of blood in her ears. But the sweep of lights passing by on the road shocked Holly back to conscious thought. She pulled away and stared at the car speeding down the road. Good grief, what if people drove by and saw them on the porch. Thank goodness for the darkness.

"We need to stop," she said, straightening her top and sliding off his lap.

Seven

Cache dragged his hands through his hair, warily trying to judge Holly's mood in the darkness.

She sat on the swing, her feet firmly on the porch, her face averted.

"I think it might be best if you go now," she said softly, watching the tail-lights of the car as it continued away.

"No one saw us. I wouldn't put your reputation on the line."

"I know. Still, it's late."

She was embarrassed. She enjoyed his kisses and lost herself in his touch. She didn't care at the moment if the entire town saw them. Except–she was too confused to know how she felt.

"Are you okay?" he asked.

She nodded. "I'm okay."

She still felt sad she couldn't have saved the horse, but knew if Cache and Sam had thought the mare was beyond help she must have been.

On the other hand, Holly felt more alive than ever because of the kisses she and Cache had shared. Lightly she traced her lips with her tongue. She still tasted of Cache McKendrick. Her heart rate was still up and it was all she could do to keep from throwing herself into his arms again.

"Holly…" Cache stopped.

What was there to say? He'd come over because he was concerned about her being upset and instead almost made love to her on the front porch.

"Goodnight, Cache." Her voice was soft, gentle in the night breeze.

He stood, then turned quickly and stooped for a kiss. His lips barely brushed across hers before he straightened and strode to his truck, never looking back.

She was only here a few months. She'd made that clear. And he thought he was clear on never trusting a relationship again. He'd been devastated when Trish died. Falling in love with someone else didn't fit into any plans he had. He couldn't go through something like that again and survive.

Cache was not at the ranch when Holly drove in the next morning. She finished her paperwork concerning Sunlight, stalling as long as she could in case he'd show up. Finally she had to leave to do the rest of the visits she had scheduled for the day.

It remained hot. The temperature rose into the triple digits and the air was still. The grass grew drier, bleached almost white, and reflected the heat of the fiery sun. The night had been warm, unusual for this part of the state where usually the evenings cooled off and made sleeping bearable.

Though it hadn't only been the heat that kept Holly awake last night. Thoughts of Cache had filled her mind, questions about Trish, about him. About them.

She went through her appointments as quickly as she could, longing to return home and change into something cool. She'd get a large drink of iced tea, find some shade and collapse. It was too hot to be working in the sun. How did the cowboys do it day after day?

When Holly returned home it was late afternoon. She was worn out. Dealing with sick or injured large animals wasn't the easiest occupation in the world.

When those same animals were fractious with the heat, it was even more difficult.

Emmie met her with a large glass of lemonade, ice tinkling against the sides. Holly gave her a grateful grin and took a big gulp.

"Heavenly!" she declared.

"If this heat doesn't break soon, I'll be a prune," Emmie complained as they entered the house. "I should have insisted Doc Watson put air-conditioning in. He doesn't care, he's gone all day. I'm surprised his wife doesn't insist."

"You get my vote if that helps. Maybe I'll pick up a window air conditioner for the office at least," Holly said.

She finished the lemonade and put down the glass, glancing through the mail stacked on the desk.

"It's supposed to stay hot for another couple of days. And nights. That's the worst part," Emmie grumbled.

Holly nodded absently as she tossed the mail back and moved towards her room.

"I for one am going to change into shorts and try to get cool."

"Take a cool shower, that'll help. I'm off now. Call if you need anything tonight. You still going up with Cache and his crew next week for the vaccinations?"

Holly paused by her door. "Still plan to. I hope it cools before that."

Or would Cache prefer to have Stan now that he had seen her reaction to a crisis?

She tried so hard to prove her worth, only to fail at the first emergency.

Holly went to bed early, to make up for the restless sleep from the previous night. But she couldn't fall asleep. First she was hot. Even with the fan on.

Then she couldn't control her thoughts. They centered on a certain roguish cowboy who constantly invaded her mind.

She tried to think about returning to Kentucky, envision her uncle's face when she arrived—only to have Cache's face dance before her eyes, with his amused eyes and lop-sided grin that set her pulses pounding.

She tried to picture her uncle's final capitulation to her request to work as a vet for Windmere Farms—only to remember Cache's arms around her as they danced, his teasing voice, the way he always called her "darlin".

And how he'd come to her after Sunlight's death to comfort her when he needed more comfort than she did.

"Which means precisely nothing," she said aloud. He was a kind man. There was nothing special going on between them. Hadn't he called Sally Lambert sugar?

He was a flirt and a charmer and Holly had best keep that in mind.

The phone rang. She reached for the extension by her bed, glancing at the clock as she did so. It was only ten. It felt much later.

"Hello, Doc?"

Cache.

"Yes." Her heart began racing. She sat up, conscious of her scanty attire.

He couldn't see her, for heaven's sake.

"Are you as hot there as we are out here, darlin'?" His voice was sweet seduction in her ear.

Holly smiled, she couldn't help it. She felt his tone like a physical caress throughout her body.

"It's hot," she replied.

"Come on out here and we'll go riding; we'll cool off some once we get away from the flat land and climb a hill or two."

"Cache, it's late. I'm already in bed."

"I'll come there, if you'd rather," he said quickly.

She grinned, for a moment letting her imagination sparkle with that picture. Reluctantly she denied herself that pleasure.

"No."

"Maybe another time."

"I doubt it."

"Now, darlin', you know we have to start making those exciting memories for you to carry back to Kentucky with you."

She laughed softly at his nonsense.

"All right, I'll come for a quick ride," she said, her heart speeding up at the thought.

"I can come and get you if you like," he suggested.

"No, I'll drive out in half the time. I'll be there soon."

"I'll have the horses waiting."

When Holly drove into the yard of the ranch, she saw him sitting on the fence near the two horses. They were saddled and ready to go and briefly Holly wondered what they must think of getting all tacked up in the middle of the hot night. For her part she felt excited beyond expectation.

In only a few minutes, they were mounted and urging the horses up the trail beside the house, heading for the open range.

"It'll be cooler by the river," Cache said, taking the lead. It was dark; only the light of the stars shed illumination. The horses walked surely, deliberately over the known trail, moving towards the faraway river.

When the trail widened, Holly moved up to ride beside Cache. She knew she was playing with fire, but was drawn to him like a moth to a flame.

"Tell me something about Kentucky and the allure it has for you, darlin'," Cache said. "Your folks live there?"

Holly blinked, startled to find his thoughts dwelling on Kentucky.

"My uncle lives there and my cousins. My parents are dead. They died when I was quite small. My uncle Tyson raised me as if I'd been his daughter."

"He owns a farm?" Obviously Cache remembered their talk on the way to the dance.

"He owns Windmere Farms. He raises thoroughbred

horses, races some."

"And that's where you want to work?"

"Yes, if he'll let me."

"Why wouldn't he?"

Holly could see that Cache was trying to see her in the night. His head was turned towards her, but it was likely he could only see her silhouette, just as that was all she could see of him.

She sighed. "Uncle Tyson believes a woman should be doing things like shopping, going to teas or hosting charity balls. Not getting dirty working with horses. When I was small, he'd let me exercise them, but once I was in high school he tried to curtail all that activity. I had to be ladylike and not worry myself about horses." Unconsciously she mimicked her uncle's words.

Some of the anger and bitterness that Holly felt seeped into her voice. Cache picked it up.

"Yet he let you become a vet." His voice was gentle.

"No, he didn't. I had to wait until I was twenty-one, then go off to college on my own. I paid my way through school. He was angry I left and refused to help thinking I'd give up and come back to host parties he gives."

"Quite an accomplishment on your part. Vet school isn't easy or cheap."

Holly nodded. It had been an accomplishment and one of which she was justifiably proud even if she had a mountain of student loan debts.

"So what does your uncle say now?" Cache asked, reining in his horse as they reached the river.

"Nothing. I haven't spoken to him since I left seven years ago."

She looked at the glimmer of stars reflected on the slow-moving water and sighed.

"I'm hoping when I show up with a degree and some experience that he'll let me work there. It's not a given, though. But family should count for something."

Cache dismounted and dropped his reins. The horse was trained to stand. He moved to Holly's side and looked up at her.

"I'll give references, if you like."

"Even after the scene I made last night?"

She tried to see his expression, but his hat blocked even the faint starlight. "I wasn't even sure you'd still want me to go on the cattle trip."

"Yes, I want you."

Cache reached up and assisted her from the horse, sliding her body down the length of his on the way. Holly's hands rested on his shoulders for balance. They felt the strength of his muscles, his heat through the cotton shirt. She was instantly aware of him as her body skimmed his, flaring into desire, heating up the hot night.

Holly pulled back, stumbled, and recovered her balance. She turned to gaze at the water, trying to keep her racing thoughts under control.

"It's still hot, though a little cooler here," she said. "I wish we had a breeze." Anything to cool down.

"Want to go swimming?" Cache stood where she'd left him, not moving to follow her as she strolled casually a few steps along the bank.

"I didn't bring a suit," she said.

He chuckled. "Neither did I. We can go skinny-dipping."

"With nothing on?"

Her voice was horrified as she turned to stare at him. She'd never done such a thing in her life.

Cache chuckled again. "It isn't as if we could see anything, it's dark as a cave out here, darlin'."

Holly shook her head. "I couldn't."

Cache moved swiftly until he was right in front of her, looking down at her. "Are you a prude or just shy?"

She thought a moment, then raised her face to his.

"I don't think I'm a prude," she said softly.

"Well, it isn't as if either of us will see anything we haven't seen before," he said gently, his hands moving to her shoulders, kneading her muscles.

"I might," she whispered, heat washing through her face.

Cache's hands stilled. The silence went on and on.

Holly thought she'd have to say something, move, do something to break the tension that seemed to be rising.

"Holly, have you ever slept with a man?" Cache's voice was low and intense, his hands tightened on her shoulders.

Holly shook her head. "No," she said, looking over towards the river.

Cache moved away from her, his thoughts in turmoil. She was in her late twenties and a virgin! His gut tightened and the longing he felt for her the other day surged again. He looked up to the stars as if seeking guidance.

He wanted her, he couldn't deny that.

But not if she was leaving soon. That wouldn't be fair to her. To either of them.

"The water sounds cool spilling over the pebbles by the edge," she said softly, longing to change the subject.

"Keep on your underwear, I'll keep mine on. In this light, or lack there of, it'll be as good as bathing suits," Cache suggested, turning back towards her.

His heart was touched she was trusting him when if she really knew what he wanted, she'd run as fast as she could.

It was hot. And in the darkness, as long as he kept his hands off her, they'd be okay in the water.

"Fine."

Holly moved back towards the horses, anxious to put distance between her and Cache, glad for the respite where she could swim and cool off and not have to discuss anything.

The water was a shock. It was cold after the heat of the night. Holly plunged into the deep part in the center where Cache indicated. The water was over her head. The current was slow, and she had no trouble floating along as it moved westward. Soon her feet touched gravel and sand and she stood, submerged to her neck. It was heavenly as her body cooled and became used to the water.

"It's great!" she called to Cache.

"Knew it would be."

He ducked under the water and soon bobbed up near her. Shaking his head to free it from the water, he sprayed Holly.

"Stop," she laughed, feeling as carefree as a child.

"Why, darlin', don't you want to get wet? It'll cool you down."

He splashed water over her again.

Holly hadn't been raised with all her male cousins for nothing. She retaliated, skimming her hand along the surface, sending a sheet of water over Cache.

In only seconds they were joined in a water battle like she hadn't enjoyed since she was a kid. She laughed and splashed and tried to avoid the sheets of water he sent her way. A couple of times she got a mouthful of water, which she spat out then splashed back even harder.

Finally she felt she'd drown if she couldn't avoid his attacks. Laughing, she held up her hands, half turned away from him to keep the water from her nose.

"Stop, stop, I surrender."

She laughed as the waves of water diminished then ceased.

"Unconditionally?" Cache demanded, moving slowly through the water towards her, his tone teasing, laughter clearly heard.

"Yes. I'll drown if I don't."

He caught her around the waist and brought her up against his chest, his face on a level with hers. Holly smiled at him, let her feet go and floated in the water, held firm against Cache.

It seemed the most natural thing in the world for Holly to wrap her arms around his neck and kiss him. Her lips touched his tentatively, but when Cache stood still and let her set the pace she increased her pressure, wanting him to respond. And he didn't disappoint her.

In only seconds, he'd assumed control and moved against her lips in a clearly sensual move. The kiss went on and on.

Holly grew warm in the cool water, her mouth craving more of his touch, more of his attention, her lips giving back as good as she got, moving against his, tasting him, touching him.

When Cache eased her away from him, the cool water swirled between them, cooling her instantly. She opened her eyes and stared up at him. Why had he stopped?

"Are you getting cold?" he asked, walking towards the bank.

"Yes."

She was now that he was no longer pressed against her.

"Get dressed; we'll ride back and have a drink or something before you go."

He kept his hand on her arm to help her up the bank, but his touch was impersonal, his mood distracted.

Holly wondered what had happened to change so suddenly. One moment kissing her and the next nothing.

If he had second thoughts, he needn't explain them to her. She'd get dressed, thank him for the refreshing ride, and return home.

They said little as they rode back. Holly worried over what had happened to change his feelings. Was it because she was a virgin? Did he only dally with accomplished flirts?

A small knot of sadness grew in her chest. She knew she wasn't offering any kind of lasting relationship. Still, she enjoyed spending time with him. She'd hate for that to be cut short before she left.

Enjoyed was too anemic. She relished spending time with him. He was exciting, stimulating, and challenging. He was more than she was used to dealing with, but she'd held her own so far.

When they reached the corral, Cache dismounted easily and reached up for her reins. "I'll unsaddle them. No point in you getting hot and dusty after your swim."

She slid off and relinquished the reins.

"Thank you for inviting me." She smiled shyly, reluctant to end the evening. She didn't know what'd gone wrong between them. Maybe she should find out.

"Goodnight, Doc." He turned and led the horses into the barn.

"Cache, wait." Holly hurried after him. "What went wrong?"

"Nothing, go on home."

She pulled on his arm, stopping him and turning him a little.

"I want to know what changed."

He stared down at her, his expression hard to read in the faint starlight. For a long moment he said nothing, then he leaned over until his face was almost touching hers.

"I'll tell you, then, darlin'. I'm a man and you're a woman. A beautiful woman, with your soft curves and your shiny brown hair that frames your face like enchantment. I lied. Wearing underwear is nothing like a swimsuit. I want you in the most primitive way I know. Having your body against mine in the river was torment beyond what I can stand. You stay away from me, Holly. I want you more than anything, and if you hang around I make no promises of platonic friendship. That's something you can count on." His face was serious.

Holly stared at him, dumbfounded. She was shocked by

his words, by the intensity of his feelings. She felt the tension in his arm, his muscles taut and tight.

She snatched her hand away as if it were burnt. Her heart pounded in her chest, the blood roared in her ears. She'd never considered something like this. She was attracted to him as she'd never been to anyone before. It thrilled her to think he was equally attracted to her.

Nothing could come of it.

Slowly she turned and walked towards her car, her head held high, her heart pounding.

"Run away, little girl," Cache called softly after her. "Be warned if you come back."

Holly drove home, his words echoing over and over. She should have known he'd want more than a few chaste kisses. And if he hadn't held back she'd probably have given him more.

The thought frightened her. She was not someone who went in for casual sex. She wanted love, commitment and the promise of a long life together.

She touched her lips lightly. He had given her memories to take down the years.

The heat spell broke the next day with a terrific thunderstorm. The rain was fierce but brief and the temperature dropped twenty degrees.

Holly worked through the worst of the storm, assisting at a breech birth. The rain reminded her of the water fight she and Cache had indulged in the night before.

Immediately she remembered what he'd said afterwards.

For the next few days she avoided any place she thought he might be, avoided anyone who worked with him. Holly didn't want to give him any reason to suspect she was reconsidering or that she acquiesced in his intentions.

She couldn't keep all thoughts of them together at bay. She wondered what it would be like to have him kiss her all over, to have his hands caress her skin, bringing her to the edge of ecstasy and beyond, to have him initiate her in the rites of love.

No, no, no! She slammed the door on such fantasies. She was leaving heart-whole and no charming cowboy was going to change that for her.

"Doc, Cache called from the Lone Tree, they leave the in the morning and he has gear you can use, but you need to have enough vaccine for forty calves," Emmie said when Holly returned from her rounds on Tuesday.

"Should I call him back?" Holly asked, anticipation building.

Despite his warning, he still expected her to go. Not that anything could happen. There'd be cowboys galore on the trip. They'd probably never have a single moment alone.

"Yes. I've packed Doc Watson's travel medical bag for you. It's got straps to go on the pack horse. And I got the duffel bag he uses when he goes. It's pretty rough in the high country, no modern conveniences." She narrowed her eyes at Holly. "You sure you're up to it?"

"I've done this before."

At least the camping part.

And the inoculations.

Just not both at the same time.

Holly longed to call Cache, to speak to him after so many days. But she hesitated, unsure of her reception. Not that she expected him to discuss anything but business, she told herself.

"Shall I call him to let him know you got the message?" Emmie asked.

"I'll call Cache as soon as I write up the files."

She moved to the desk and opened the first patient's file.

Emmie left before Holly was finished. Holly put off her call, forcing herself to finish all the updates before calling.

She felt nervous when she dialed, her stomach churning as the phone rang. The let-down was almost physical when Sam answered.

"I was calling about the trip to the summer pasture," Holly said.

"Sure thing, Doc. We leave at sun-up tomorrow. Cache said to tell you to bring a soft-sided suitcase for your clothes, to dress in layers and he'll take care of the rest. Grub and sleeping bag and all."

"I'll be there by five."

Disappointment warred with excitement as Holly hung up.

She hadn't spoken to Cache, but tomorrow she'd see him! Spend several days in his company, working beside him, resting in the evenings with him and his men.

She smiled in anticipation. No matter what, she was excited to be going.

It was a few minutes before five when Holly pulled into the yard at the Lone Tree the next morning.

Yet by the activity going on, she wondered if she was late. Men were everywhere, saddling horses, loading supplies on a serviceable chuck wagon, piling sleeping gear in another wagon, herding horses to swap with when their own mounts grew tired.

Holly no sooner stopped her truck than Cache opened her door and smiled at her.

"Morning, darlin", you look fresh as a daisy. Ready for this trek?"

None of the frustration or warning from the other evening showed in his face.

Her heart pounded and her eyes shone in her happiness at the day as she nodded. He was dressed in a faded checked shirt, faded blue jeans and old leather chaps. His boots were worn and scuffed but still had years of use ahead.

"Where do you want all my gear?" she asked, still sitting as he was blocking her.

"Tim!" Cache roared.

In only a second one of his hands loped over.

"Take Doc's gear, will you?"

Cache pointed to the duffel bag in the truck bed.

"And the medical supplies?" she asked. That container was beside her on the front seat.

"That'll go in the chuck wagon. Anything need refrigeration?"

When Holly shook her head, Cache told Tim to come back for the medical bag. He stepped back and Holly got out.

She wore an old pair of jeans, her boots and a cotton T-shirt beneath a flannel shirt. Her new hat would get a workout this trip. The morning was cool, now that the heat spell had broken, and while she knew she wouldn't need the flannel shirt later it felt good now. She had a jacket and sweatshirt in her duffel in case it got cold at night where they were going.

"I'm ready." She smiled with excitement.

Cache smiled back, teasing lights in his eyes. He reached out and pulled the stampede strap beneath her chin, cinching it snug. "We'll be doing some hard riding this morning. You don't want to lose it."

Holly felt the tingling awareness that his fingers generated rush through her. She licked her lips hoping he didn't see her heart beating, didn't notice her erratic breathing.

Dear God, how would she last a week?

"Ready when you are, boss," a hand called.

"Right. Mount up." Cache nodded towards Beau. "Your horse, darlin". Let's go."

Holly was caught up in the excitement as a half dozen cowboys, a chuck wagon and a remuda of horses began moving out to the open range and towards the high summer pastures where the cattle grazed.

A spot several miles in the distance would be their first stop. After inoculating the calves, they'd move farther west.

Holly had been on one cattle drive before, so she knew how strenuous the work was. Yet there was a tremendous satisfaction in the process which had changed little in the last one hundred years. She was looking forward to being a part of it.

As they spread out across the open range, the men driving the horses moved out ahead as all the horses wanted to run. Holly moved to the side to let them by and tried to avoid their dust, content to ride at a slower pace.

She wasn't alone. Two or three others ambled along at a slow lope, rather than the hell-for-leather gait of the leaders. Sam rode over to her and told her a little about the set-up to which they were headed.

Before too long, Cache came riding back from the lead. He pulled in beside them, discussing work with Sam, pointing out landmarks to Holly.

They stopped for a quick lunch, then started out again. Holly was content to be in the rear, able to watch all that was taking place in front of her. She could relax until they reached the summer pastures. Her work hadn't started.

As the afternoon waned, she grew restless and sore from the long unaccustomed hours in the saddle. She'd be glad for the evening's rest.

According to Cache, they were to reach their campground around six. That'd be their base for the next few days. She wouldn't need to ride so much tomorrow as the cowboys would bring the calves to her, cutting out the ones that needed shots. She only had to finish today without giving away how much she wanted to stop.

Holly had earlier discarded her flannel shirt, tying it to the back of her saddle. She wished she could discard her shirt. It was hot. She was hot. Sunscreen on her arms kept her from burning, but she longed for some shade.

Cache joined her as they began climbing. The terrain rose

toward the high pasture.

"I'm going to sweep through some of those canyons to the left, Sam's going right. Want to ride along?"

"Sure."

She turned to follow him, her fatigue forgotten. She'd ride anywhere with Cache.

The sagebrush grew to the height of Holly's knees even sitting on Beau. As they wound their way through some of the thick sage, branches slapped against her legs, pulled her jeans as if trying to dislodge her.

She knew why Cache wore the chaps. Maybe she'd get some before doing anything like this again.

If she ever did anything like this again.

There was nothing like this in Kentucky.

Cache spotted a couple of heifers and headed in their direction, turning them and the calves with them towards the base camp, steering them in their slow, ambling way. Once they were started, he continued on, eyes constantly searching the terrain for more.

"What if they turn around?" Holly asked as she pushed Beau to catch up.

"They'll probably drift, but they'll be headed generally in the right direction. We'll check out this canyon, then double back and keep them on track. You holding up okay?"

"I'm doing okay."

He smiled and nodded. "You'll do."

With a nudge, Roman started forward.

They searched one canyon, then moved to another. Several times Holly spotted the red coat of the cattle and moved to push them in the direction of the camp. Several were yearlings. Others had calves hustling to keep up with their mother.

Cache seemed tireless and Holly pushed herself to keep up with him. She hoped she could hold her own.

She swung wide, looking for more cattle. In one of the gullies they crisscrossed, she spotted three. Urging Beau down, they started across the dry stream bed, heading for the cattle. Loping along, suddenly Beau stumbled. Caught off guard, Holly slipped from the saddle, over his head, landing hard on the rocky ground.

Eight

Holly held on to consciousness as blackness around the edge of her vision faded back to daylight. She saw Beau standing a few feet away.

Assessing her situation, she realized the banks of the gully rose above her to hide any sign of her from a distance. Where was Cache? She lay perfectly still for a moment. Except for a roaring headache, she seemed to be in one piece. Gingerly she tried sitting up.

The pounding of Roman's hoofs shook the dry ground and Holly looked over her shoulder to see Cache riding hard. He was out of his saddle in seconds, kneeling beside her.

"Are you all right?"

His face mirrored his concern, his fear.

"I think so. My head's killing me, but I don't think I broke anything. Is Beau okay?"

"I don't know, we'll check him in a moment. What happened?"

He reached down to gently draw her to her feet, watching to make sure she could stand before turning to glance at Beau.

"I thought you said you could ride," he teased her, his eyes twinkled in amusement, relief evident in his expression as she walked slowly over to the horse standing patiently watching them.

"Ohhh!" She flared up and turned on him, her hands on hips. "Of course I can ride. I wasn't expecting him to throw me. Neither was Beau. Thanks for your concern."

Cache's expression instantly became serious. "I was concerned, how can you doubt that? I was just teasing. Let's see how Beau is."

"I'm sorry, Cache, I didn't mean to snap. My head hurts."

She brushed back a few tendrils of hair that drifted around her face, discovering the small lump where she'd hit the ground.

"I'm surprised you came out of the saddle, stumble or not. I've seen you ride. You're good."

He reached the horse and rested his hand on his rump, running his hands down his legs each in turn.

Holly ran her hands over Beau's forelegs. She winced at the swelling she felt on the left foreleg.

"Does it hurt, old fellow?" she said softly, her hands gentle as she assessed the damage.

She turned to Cache. "I think it's a bad sprain. He must have stepped into a chuckhole. It doesn't feel broken, but he shouldn't walk any more than he has to. And definitely not be ridden for a few days. How far are we from camp?"

Cache looked back the way they'd come.

"A couple of hours, maybe, walking. If someone doesn't come looking for us, I don't know how far Roman can carry us both. He's had a full day already and you know it's not an easy trail back to camp."

He didn't have to say it was even further back to the ranch. Holly knew how much distance they'd covered that day. And how rough and uneven the terrain had been.

"I don't think Beau should stress that leg. You ride back, get help and come back for me."

She wasn't worried about being alone for a few hours. There was plenty of daylight left.

"It'll be dark before I could get back. I might miss you and you'd be out all night alone. It'll get cold tonight. I'm not leaving you. We'll hope one of the men rides this way. Otherwise we'll wait for morning."

As if to prove his words, a slight breeze blew across Holly's face, the air cooler that what she'd been feeling all afternoon. There was very little shelter in the open canyon. Some gullies which wouldn't provide much protection.

They were some distance from the slope of the rim and the open space in front of them allowed the wind free access. Around them was only the dried grass and silvery sage of the high desert. Nothing to shelter from a breeze if it picked up. Nothing to hold in warmth.

"Is that all you have to keep warm?" Cache looked at her T-shirt.

"My flannel shirt's tied on the saddle. I'll be all right."

She'd probably be wishing for her sweatshirt before tomorrow. The flannel shirt would just have to do. It wasn't going to get cold enough to do any harm–just be uncomfortable.

"We're at a higher elevation than town. And that heat spell

broke. It'll get cold up here tonight. Let's find a place to hole up."

He loosened Beau's saddle and then reached for his bridle as he walked back towards Roman.

"We can ride double for a short distance. We'll ride towards the hills and look for a sheltered place for protection from the night wind. Beau can go that far, can't he?" Cache asked.

She nodded, not wanting to leave the horse on his own. She watched as he grabbed Roman's reins and easily swung into his saddle. When he was set, he motioned for Holly to come closer, then leaned over so far she thought he'd fall off, reached down his hands and clasped them beneath her arms. Holly was conscious of his warmth against her sides, his palms skimming the edge of her breasts. She took a breath. Now was not the time to be thinking of such a thing. She had to get on the horse.

"On three, spring up," he said, his voice low and calm.

She nodded, her hands on his arms, her eyes on his. All she could think of was his hands against her body, the warmth emanating from them.

"…three."

Springing up, Holly was pulled up to sit sideways in front of Cache. He slid back as far as he could go and she swung her leg over the horse's neck and sank into the valley between the saddle horn and Cache's strong thighs. His right arm came round beneath her breasts and took up the reins. His left hand held Beau's reins.

Holly held herself as stiffly as possible, not wanting to give in to the urge to lean against him, to feel the strong muscles of his chest support her. The warmth of his legs and arm were almost more than she could tolerate. Her body longed for his. What would he do if she turned around and kissed him?

She wanted to feel his mouth against hers again, to feel his hands touching her, to explore the pleasure he could offer.

She tried to hold herself stiffly away as if that would lessen temptation.

"Relax." He shook her gently. "You're too stiff. Move with Roman."

Cache pulled her back against his chest as the horses began walking, picking their way through the sage, over the rocks heading towards the ridge, slowly so that Beau could keep up without further stress to his injury.

Holly tried to relax and move with the horse, but she could only think of the man holding her. His chest muscles moved against her back as he directed the horse, kept Beau's reins firmly in hand. The heat of his arm sent tingling waves of awareness throughout. Her bottom rested against his thighs and she could feel those muscles move as he guided Roman.

Shifting slightly, trying to put distance between them, she gradually became aware of the change in Cache. She froze.

"Darlin'", you've got to sit still. I get hard just thinking about you and with your soft little bottom moving around like that I'm more than thinking about you."

"Sorry."

Her voice came out squeaky. Her body shot through with heat and the pictures that flooded her mind were X-rated. What would happen if she gave into the desire that sprang up between them whenever they were close to one another?

The excitement of the cattle trip was forgotten. Even Windmere Farms was forgotten as Holly could only envision being with the man she rode with. For a few moments she let her mind take off in a flight of fantasy, only to jerk herself up short when she realized where her thoughts were leading. Dangerous thoughts. She had to remember her life's goals!

She shifted a little and heard Cache groan behind her.

"You're driving me crazy!" he said in a half groan half laugh.

"Sorry," she said again, swallowing hard.

Did he even wonder what he was doing to her!

"I didn't mean to drive you crazy," she added softly.

"Here we are, you plastered as close to me as you can get with clothes on, your legs against mine, your soft bottom doing crazy things to me."

Holly was drowning in sensations. Her heart pounded and heat flooded. Where was the cool night breeze when she needed it?

She couldn't talk, only relax back against him a little, as if encouraging him in his pursuit.

Cache's hand nuzzled the edge of her shirt, slipping beneath it to slowly stroke the soft skin covering her ribs. Holly caught her breath. The sensations were exquisite, delightful. She wanted more. Opening her mouth for better ventilation, she sighed softly and relaxed completely against him.

Roman stumbled. Cache gripped the horse with his legs and pulled his hand from beneath her shirt.

"We've gone far enough. He's tired and I don't want him to get injured." Cache said, pulling the horse to a stop.

"Right."

She could scarcely speak. She felt like her bones had melted.

"Swing your leg over his neck," Cache said.

In only seconds, Holly was on the ground. She reached for Beau's reins and checked the horse's leg. It was hot where it was swollen and she wished she had something cool to put on it.

Cache dismounted next to her. All business, all cowboy, he turned to care for his horse first.

Holly followed suit and unsaddled Beau. She checked his leg again, noting the swelling and the scrape on his leg. There was nothing further she could do without her medical bag. She wished she'd brought it with her but never expected something like this.

She carried the saddle towards the large flat rock. It held the warmth from the afternoon sun and felt good on her back when she sat beside the saddle and leaned against the rock.

"Now what?" she asked.

Cache put Roman's saddle beside Beau's.

"Now we wait for morning. We may go hungry, but we both have canteens of water, so we won't go thirsty."

Cache went to work gathering and piling some dead branches of sage near them to build a small fire.

"When it gets going good, it'll give us some heat which will also reflect back from that rock. It should be warm enough through the night we won't be too uncomfortable," he said as he worked.

"If we have a big enough fire any of the men who might be scouting for us will see the fire and head this way."

"Is that standard if someone is late getting to camp? Others ride out to look for them" she asked.

"Probably not. I read it in a western once."

"And do you read a lot of westerns?" she asked, curious about his reading habits.

Actually, she was curious about every aspect of Cache McKendrick.

Cache looked up, his eyes looking deep into hers and his head slowly shook. "I like them well enough. But generally don't have a lot of reading time except in winter. What do you like?"

"Mysteries. Actually what's called cozy mysteries where regular people solve the murder not cops."

They discussed various authors and then segued into movies. Twilight came, then night.

Holly put on her flannel shirt and sat close to him. He pulled her closer, his arm around her shoulder."

"In another time or place, we might have something going for us," Cache said as she rested her head on his shoulder.

"But I don't want to spoil things when you head back to Kentucky to find that special unending romance," he said, watching her from beneath the brim of his hat.

"I'm going back to be a vet at Windmere Farms. If I find a special unending relationship, so much the better."

She tilted her chin at him.

"What if it's all changed?" he asked gently.

She'd never considered that.

She'd been cut off from communications for seven years.

What if things had changed? What if there wasn't a place for her on Windmere?

"I don't know. I'm hoping my uncle will let me work there. I don't know what I'll do if he still says no. I've been planning this for seven years." Holly smiled a little. "It's been my driving goal for so long–work as the primary vet for Windmere Farms–I don't have a fall back plan."

"You'd find another goal," he said.

"Hmm, maybe."

She fell silent, not wanting to think along those lines.

For a moment she was scared. What if things had changed? What if her uncle no longer owned the farm? Or worse, what if he hadn't changed one iota and was as intractable as he'd been before still believing she should go to dinners and dances and not mess about the stables?

Holly was surprised to find that the thought didn't upset her as much as it used to. Nor as much as she thought it should.

Cache was right, she'd find another goal.

Had she grown up somewhere along the way?

She'd still be a vet–and a good one. She'd be able to work with horses or cattle, or whatever took her fancy.

She slanted a look at Cache from beneath her lashes. He wanted her. She knew that. But he never said anything about loving.

Would it make a difference to her if he loved her?

Her heart sped up and her stomach suddenly felt full of butterflies. Ruthlessly she damped down the thought. She wasn't going to fall for some cowboy, no matter how sexy.

"What about you, Cache? If Trish died so long ago, why haven't you married again?"

He flicked her a glance.

"I don't plan to marry again. It didn't work so well the first time."

"You can't help that she died," she said, surprised at his answer.

She wished he'd tell her something about his wife. About their lives together. Had he loved her so much there was no room to love anyone else?

He sighed and looked back at the fire. He was silent so long she thought he wasn't going to speak again.

"You remind me a little of Trish. Except she was more at home at dances and nightclubs and the concert halls than on a ranch. She pined for the city. We were happy at first, but after a few months she grew discontented and bored. We didn't have much money back then, so I couldn't afford to give her the trips she wanted."

"No one has money starting out."

Holly remembered how long he'd owned the ranch—only a decade. He'd done so much it was hard to remember he'd done it in that short time.

"It sounds practical now when you say it, but she didn't want to be practical. She wanted bright lights and fun and excitement. It's hard trying to build up a ranch. Exhausting when so much of the work had to be done without help. There are plenty of men, now, on the ranch. But even today I don't have a lot of cash. Like most ranchers I'm cash poor and land rich. But I can't spend dirt. I'm doing better now than we ever did while she was alive. I wanted to give her the moon. But towards the end she was so unhappy. And all I ever wanted was to make her happy."

Her heart ached for him. He must have loved her so much. She could hear the hurt in his voice.

"Everyone thought we were the perfect couple, young, starting out with some amazing breaks going our way, happy. But it was a facade. We had some real yelling matches."

He looked over at Holly. "I haven't told many people this, but she was killed when she was leaving me."

She widened her eyes in shock. She'd never expected that!

Cache saw her startled look and shrugged, turning back to the fire, his face set in bitter lines.

"So, knowing I can't make a woman happy, I'm not going to even try again. I've got a younger brother. He or his kids can inherit the ranch when I'm gone," he said.

Holly didn't know what to say. It sounded like Trish had been a bit spoiled and immature. Even if things had gone wrong in their marriage, it didn't mean Cache shouldn't have another shot. Maybe he'd find someone to love who'd love him back and not care a whit about money or bright lights.

She'd thought he'd loved Trish so much that he couldn't bear to look at another woman. The reality was quite different.

Cache wasn't avoiding other women because he couldn't forget Trish. He was avoiding involvement to avoid a situation like he'd had with Trish.

"Not all women are like Trish. You could find someone else who loved ranching. Who had the same expectations you have, the same commitment to making the Lone Pine Ranch grow and flourish. There're lots of women who'd love to live on a ranch."

She almost mentioned Sally, but drew the line there.

"You for one?" he challenged her.

For a moment Holly felt her heart leap. Was he suggesting she stay?

Or only trying to prove a point when she said no.

Was the dream of the last seven years worth it? If he asked her to stay, would she consider it?

Before she could seriously answer the question, he spoke again.

"Forget it, darlin". It was a rhetorical question anyway. Are you warm enough?"

He moved away to toss some more branches on the fire.

"Yes, thank you."

The sky was dark. The only light they had was from the fire and the stars. Holly rubbed her arms.

It was cooler now. How much colder would it get before dawn?

"Sorry there's no food," he said.

"Well since neither one of us expected this, I'm not surprised," she said, watching the greedy flames attack the dry wood.

The warmth felt good. Holly looked across the fire at Cache, wondering how badly had he been hurt by Trish. He had some happy memories. Did he cling to those. Was he wishing they'd made more happy memories before it all changed?

Was that why he was talking to her about making happy memories?

They were all he had left of his marriage. Which was really sad.

Was he serious in never wanting another try at love, because that hadn't worked?

If she loved someone, she'd do anything she could to be with him, make him happy. But if it didn't work out, would she turn her back on other chances?

She stared into the flames, trying to find the answer.

"You'll go blind, staring into the light," Cache said, watching the flickering light on her face.

Holly looked up and stuck out her tongue.

"You sound like a mother. I'm fine. People gaze into fires all the time. They're mesmerizing. Besides, it's the only light. Where else should I look?"

I could look at you, she thought, all night.

"Tell me about your uncle and your cousins," Cache said. He came back and sat beside her, putting his arm around her shoulders.

"If you tell me about your folks and your brother who stands to inherit your vast ranch."

Cache chuckled at that. "Hardly vast. But sure, I'll let you in on all the family secrets."

For the next few hours they shared stories about their families, finding some surprising similarities and expected differences.

Holly was pleased to note as the evening progressed her headache gradually faded. She touched the bump from time to time, not sure it was going down, but at least the blinding pain was going.

Cache's family had been ranchers for generations. What was surprising was that he'd branched out on his own. His father's spread was still a going concern and he could have worked there. As his brother did.

"But I wouldn't have been top dog at least until he retired. Which will probably be never. So I got my own spread," he said.

"I'm sure you always wanted to be top dog. You could have been when you inherited your dad's ranch."

"If he lives to be ninety, I'd be in my late sixties. Too long to wait."

Holly explained her uncle's old-fashioned ideas of her being a southern belle, never dirtying her hands with stable work. Explained her frustration at not being able to do what she wanted, not being taken seriously, as her cousins were–just because they were male.

"So you plan to change all that when you go back," Cache said softly, as Holly gave a huge yawn.

She nodded, her gaze drifting back to the fire. She was warm and content. She didn't need food or a house–just warmth and this man near her.

Cache rose and picked up his saddle and dropped it between the fire and the boulder. Taking the saddle blanket in hand, he motioned to Holly.

"Lie down here. You can use the saddle as a pillow. With

the fire on one side and the boulder on the other it'll be as warm as we'll get."

"I don't want to be covered with that blanket, it smells like horse." She wrinkled her nose.

"Better than freezing to death. Besides, you've smelled worse."

His lop-sided grin tugged at her heart.

Cache sat down and patted the ground beside him. "Come on."

Watching him warily, she moved to sit beside him. "Now what?"

"We lie down." Cache lay back, his head on the saddle.

As she started to lie down, he gathered her against him, dropping the heavy horse blanket over them, his arm coming around her.

Holly felt warmer instantly.

"Is this what being a cowboy is like?" she murmured, growing sleepy now that she felt relaxed and warm.

Trying to ignore the hunger that gnawed at her stomach, she wished she'd at least brought a candy bar. This day wasn't turning out the way she'd thought it would, but maybe it was even better.

She was enjoying herself, she realized in surprise.

Cache chuckled. "Not usually. It's rare I sleep with anyone on the range."

She smiled at the thought and moved closer. In only a moment she closed her eyes, listening to the sounds of the night—the fire crackling merrily near by, the breeze rustling through the sage, soft scampering noises as the night animals went about their business.

Soon she slept.

Cache felt her relax when she fell asleep and smiled into the night. He pulled her closer, fitting her body against his from shoulder to thigh. She smelled fresh and clean even after a day of riding. If he couldn't have her the way he wanted, this would have to do.

He gazed into the night, wishing things had been different. Wishing for the moon, as his mother would say.

It was late before he slept.

When Holly awoke the next morning, Cache was up and moving around. She must have made some noise, though, because he looked over at her almost immediately.

"How're you feeling?" he asked.

The sun was already up and the early morning chill dissipated. She saw Roman bridled and standing, awaiting the saddle. Beau was near by, cropping on some weeds. Looking again at Cache, she noticed his faint beard, golden hair glinting in the sun, and smiled. Nice to wake up to.

"I'm hungry, thirsty and wish I could have a shower. Other than that I'm having fun on your camp-out."

He smiled back. "You're a good sport, Holly."

She sat up, pushing off the horse blanket with a grimace. It had kept her warm in the night, but she didn't like smelling like a horse.

"Hey, I'm your vet. This goes with the territory. You'd expect the same from Dr. Watson, wouldn't you?"

She stood up and stretched out some of the kinks. Her back was stiff from sleeping on the hard ground. She was a little surprised she'd slept as well as she had.

"I probably wouldn't have shared my saddle and blanket with that doctor," Cache said. "Let's get going. We'll see how far this old fella can take us today."

He quickly saddled Roman while Holly tacked up Beau, leaving the girth loose.

Cache scattered the remnants of the fire, making sure there were no embers.

"Ready?"

"Sure."

"You get up and then I'll get on behind you," he said, standing by the side of the horse.

Holly reached up and clasped her hands behind his head, bringing him down so that she could brush a kiss across his lips.

With a soft groan, Cache caught her mouth with his and kissed her long and hard. She was smiling when he drew back.

With a scowl, he helped her up into the saddle. Without another word, he mounted behind her, gathered Beau's reins, and set off.

Holly knew better than to press her luck, so she kept silent, but smiled in pure pleasure when his arm came around her and held her.

They'd been traveling for half an hour or so when they spotted another rider coming down the hill in the distance. It was Sam and he was leading a second horse.

"Rescued," Holly murmured. "I hope he brought food."

Cache urged Roman towards Sam and in only moments they met.

Sam knew something was wrong when Cache hadn't returned camp before dark.

He'd set out at first light to find them, bringing another horse, just in case.

"I knew you'd be okay with Cache out here," he said as he finished his explanation.

Holly wondered what okay meant. She thought about their time around the fire, the stories shared, the contentment she'd felt.

Yes, she was okay with Cache.

Without a word, Cache dismounted, assisted her down and, taking Beau's saddle, soon had Holly mounted on the new horse.

Sam tossed them each an apple and they started towards the camp. Holly kept quiet as the men talked about how many more cattle might be in the canyons and breaks around the camp.

Cache practically ignored her when they reached camp. He dismounted, letting her get off the horse herself. None of the body-to-body contact of the previous day. It was as if she were Dr. Watson, she mused as he turned away and quickly moved to check out the men and their assignments.

She hurried over to the chuck wagon, grateful for the cup of coffee the cook offered her. Her head didn't hurt today. And the coffee was like ambrosia. She drank half the cup before taking a breath. When the cook offered her a biscuit filled with ham and eggs and cheese, she ate as if she were starving. Glancing over at Cache, she felt neglected. Which was foolish. She was here to work. And so was he.

Once hunger had been satisfied, she returned to Beau, checking on his leg. The cook had some ice in the cooler and Holly made a ice pack and wrapped it around the horse's sprain. She'd keep an eye on him, but as long as he didn't run or carry anyone, he'd likely heal up as well as he would at home.

The next few days were busy. Holly inoculated the calves, checked for parasites or disease, assisted in some of the ear-notching. Once in a while she'd noticed Cache staring at her, but usually something would draw her attention and when she'd look back he'd be busy elsewhere.

Tired at the end of each day, Holly did her best to blend into the evening routines. She didn't want anyone to have a negative comment because a woman was along. She was the vet, plain and simple.

On the afternoon of the fourth day they prepared to move to another area of the range, having finished with all the cattle in that sector. She brushed out her hair after lunch, and rebraided it to hang down her back. A quick wash and she was as fresh as she was going to get until she got home.

She loaded her things in the wagon and went to get her horse. Beau had improved with rest, but she still didn't want to put him to strenuous use. She took the other horse she'd been riding–Tomahawk.

Everyone was helping break camp, saddling horses and packing up. She readied her mount, then moved out of the commotion, to the edge of the camp. They were on a high plateau and she could look over the valley and see for maybe a hundred miles. She so enjoyed her view of the open range, no sign of man anywhere.

"You look as if you just stepped from a bandbox," Cache's voice sounded behind her.

Holly spun around and smiled at him, pleased he had taken a moment to stop and talk with her—she felt she hadn't seen him for days. He came around the horse and stood next to her, his back to the view, trapping her between her horse and his own broad chest. She liked her new view better.

He wore a checked shirt, unbuttoned and hanging from his shoulders, admitting a tantalizing glimpse of his broad chest, deeply tanned from work in the sun. His beard was several days old, and looked like fine gold glinting in the sun.

Her fingers tingled with yearning to touch it, to see if it was as soft as it looked. His eyes were a deep blue, their mocking gaze evident as he looked down at her.

"Kind of you to say so. I thought you'd forgotten I was here."

Instantly she colored, angry that she'd given herself away. He was busy working, for heaven's sake, not out here to entertain her.

"Oh, no, darlin", I haven't forgotten for a single moment that you're here. Not during the day, nor during any of the long nights." His voice was low, intimate.

"It's been busy."

She floundered for something to say, keeping her eyes resolutely on his, avoiding the temptation of reaching out to touch him, though her fingers ached with desire to do that very thing.

"But not too busy to watch you. And see you watching me."

His lop-sided smile melted Holly's heart. She took a shaky breath, not wanting to end the moment.

Cache reached around her and rested his hand on her saddle, enclosing her even closer in a small world of their own. The horse shifted his weight and stood still. Cache moved closer, his head tipped down towards her so that his hat sheltered her from the sun. His eyes lost their teasing look. Instead, Holly recognized hunger in their depths.

She reached out her hand to keep him away, her fingers tantalized by the feel of his skin as her hand made contact beneath the open shirt. Without thought, she traced the muscles of his chest.

Cache drew in a sharp breath, his hands clenching, his gaze narrowing as he stared down into Holly's dreamy eyes.

"Do you know what you're doing?" he asked in a harsh voice.

She licked her lips and shook her head slightly, only knowing she didn't want to stop.

"What I'd like to do is take you off into the hills somewhere, away from all these guys, for a few hours. Just you and me. I'd strip your clothes from your delicate little body and kiss every inch of your skin. Then taste you all over, then make slow, hot love to you, until we couldn't do it any more."

Holly felt a delicious weakness invade her limbs. Her knees grew weak and her body warmed at his words. She stared into his eyes–blue pools, deep and dark and passionate, the hunger evident. Her mind took flight at the images he evoked. For a long moment she forgot about Kentucky, forgot about his reluctance to get involved with anyone. It would be glorious making love with Cache. Why not?

"When are you going to do us both a favor and sleep with me before you take yourself off to Kentucky? The memories we make will keep you warm when you get. Can you deny it?"

No, she couldn't, not without lying both to him and herself. Her fingers continued to caress the warm skin of his chest even as her mind leaped ahead to the picture he'd painted.

Theirs was not destined to be a long-term relationship. But she'd never wanted to make love with a man the way she wanted Cache McKendrick. They'd hurt no one if they slipped away. She had no one else, nor did he.

Nine

When Holly didn't respond, Cache caught her chin in his left hand and tilted her face gently, his hand slipping down to caress her throat, his thumb drawing feather-light strokes along her jaw. Slowly he lowered his head, his mouth hovering scant inches above hers, his breath mingling softly with hers. Holly could scarcely breathe.

"Tell me if you don't want me," he repeated again, then covered her lips with his before she could answer.

Holly opened her mouth and eagerly responded to his kiss as she hadn't to his question. Her tongue danced with his. She strained to get closer, moving to encircle him around his waist, her hands tracing patterns on his bare back, beneath the loose shirt. Learning him, sculpting him, wanting to get even closer. She was hot, and it had nothing to do with the sun beating down on them—this heat came from within, came from the flames Cache ignited within her.

He could feel her pulse in her throat. He kept his fingers lightly against that slender column, caressing the soft warm skin.

Though his touch was light, it was as if it paralyzed her.

She couldn't breathe, couldn't think, could only feel the sensations that roiled through her.

"Hey, boss, you going to hang around here all day?"

Cache raised his head, looked over Holly, over her horse to Sam. His expression darkened, then he took a deep breath.

"No, I'm not. Everyone ready?"

Sam nodded and glanced around. Most of the other men were already moving out, the chuck wagon had lumbered past and the few hanging around were watching Cache, knowing grins wide on their faces.

"Well dern," he said softly.

"I have enough trouble with people questioning if I'm competent as a vet without everyone in Redbud thinking I let the cowboys maul me," Holly said, ducking from under his arm and yanking the horse's reins.

She was overreacting again, she knew, but she was embarrassed to be caught with everyone watching. She needed to guard against that kind of thing, but when around Cache she forgot everything.

Cache jerked back to avoid being hit by the horse's head, then glared after her, his temper flaring.

"It takes two, darlin'. I didn't see you beating me away. Besides, everyone doesn't think you let anyone maul you. Maybe they know you're mine."

He stood straight, his legs spread apart, his fists on his hips.

"Don't be a dog in the manger, Cache," Holly said, mounting her horse then leaning over so that he could hear her and she hoped no one else could.

"You don't want me except for a toss in the hay. You don't want any long-term commitment, remember? The whole town knows that. Stay away from me. I'm here to work."

She turned and kicked the horse, taking her frustration out on that poor animal. Tomahawk started off at a swift trot and when Holly gave the sign broke into a lope. It wasn't his fault, she was mad at Cache. The man was infuriating!

But he'd made it perfectly clear he didn't want her beyond a night and that was fine with her.

She didn't have time for some dumb cowboy who was too afraid of repeating the past to give the future a chance, who judged all women by one.

One moreover who was dead and gone.

She ignored the small voice that asked what she'd been thinking of a few moments before, when he'd tried to talk her into lovemaking. How appealing it sounded, how enticing.

She was here to work and work she would. When the cattle drive was over, she'd be heart-whole and fancy-free.

But even as she rode out into the plain, a small voice inside called her a liar.

Working with the longhorns in the new section the next day proved different from with the Herefords. The descendants of early Texas cattle were not as even tempered as the Herefords. Everyone exercised more care around them than the other cattle. Holly watched carefully, did her job and stayed away from the main body of the herd and from Cache.

Every time she saw him heading in her direction, she'd latch on to Tim or Larry or Sam and start a discussion. She'd keep her attention on whatever topic they discussed, though every nerve-ending was attuned to Cache. She knew when he watched her and a small glow of satisfaction engulfed her at the thought. But she kept her distance. He was too tempting.

Cache let her get away with it, but his eyes followed her, knowing and patient. He'd stand and watch her and whomever she was talking to. Holly felt his eyes on her and tossed her head, as if she didn't have a care in the world, but he knew she knew and it amused him—when it didn't drive him crazy.

Every time she was tempted to give in and go to him, her pride reared up.

He'd been honest with her—he didn't want anything more than a toss in the hay.

And she knew better than to let herself be talked into that. At least she thought she did.

At night in her sleeping-bag, however, with the stars overhead and the fire burning merrily near by, she'd remember his soft voice, the image his words suggested when he proposed they slip away and she'd yearn for him.

Two days later the drive ended and Holly and the men headed for the ranch house and home. The last of the calves had been inoculated. It was time to wind down and return to day-to-day routine.

The pace back was slow, talk desultory among the cowboys. Even the remuda horses walked along, no longer running with fresh energy. The excitement from a week ago had dampened now with all the hard work that'd been required.

The next time they rode out everyone would start off full of energy, too, she knew. But she wouldn't be part of the team. Doc Watson would be back by then.

Holly was bone-weary. She had pushed and pulled and inoculated and notched and castrated more calves than she could count. She'd done her fair share and was satisfied with her performance. Dr. Watson couldn't have done better.

While horses were her first love, she liked working with cattle well enough, and had enjoyed herself tremendously, learned things, and felt more confident in her abilities day by day. She was glad she'd chosen her field and knew she'd continue to do well in the profession.

Now she was ready to go home–to a hot bath, a quiet house and a soft bed. Much as she liked large animals, she couldn't wait to get away from dirt and smell and hard sleeping bags. Away from the turmoil of cattle, cowboys and Cache.

"So you survived." Sam rode up beside her and reined in his horse to match her gait.

"Appears I have." She smiled at him. "And had a grand time to boot."

He chuckled, shook his head. "Hardest work there is and you had a grand time. Don't figure. But you did us proud, Doc. I'm glad you came along."

"Thanks."

She shifted a little in the saddle, trying to ease aching muscles, thinking of the long, hot soak she planned to have once she was home. Her muscles were sore, her hair gritty with dirt and dust and she was tired!

It was going to be the best appreciated bath in her life—

if she could just stay awake long enough to enjoy it!

"You and the boss getting on okay?" Sam asked after a moment.

Her head turned to him. "Why do you ask?"

"Well, he's as grouchy as an angry grizzly and you're avoiding him like he was carrying the plague." He shrugged, "Just wondering, that's all."

Sam threw her a look under his brim.

"Except for the fact your boss doesn't want to get involved with any woman, unless it's a one night stand, everything's just fine," she snapped out, angry that even though she wasn't looking for a long-term relationship either, Cache made no bones about not wanting one from her.

"He had a hard time with Trish. He's a little gun-shy."

"Well, it's time he remembered everyone's not Trish."

Sam looked at her for a long moment, then nodded his head.

"I guess you're right. Trish wouldn't have come on a drive like this, much less stuck it out. She'd never have offered to help in any way. You two ain't alike at all."

"Too bad Cache can't keep that in mind."

That was his problem. He couldn't forget Trish. It didn't help that he attributed all women to being like her.

Well, he was wrong. Not that it mattered, but he should remember that.

"Give him some time, Doc, he'll come around," Sam said.

"He can have all the time he wants, but I'm leaving once Dr. Watson returns." She said it loud and clear, almost defiantly.

Everyone needed to remember she was only here temporarily.

Especially herself.

Holly managed to avoid Cache at the ranch in all the confusion and commotion. Keeping a wary eye out as he moved among his men, gave directions and orders, she quickly unsaddled her horse and brushed him down.

Sam took care of the feed and Holly went to check Beau one last time. Satisfied that he was healing as he should be, she slipped out to get into her truck.

Eyeing it as she approached, she gave a small smile. It was dirty, dusty and looked as if it were five years old. It fit right in with the other vehicles around the barnyard and gave her a sense of belonging.

Maybe she should give it a wash, but not today.

She was gone before she saw Cache again.

The house hot and silent when she entered. There was a note from Emmie about fresh food in the refrigerator. She noted it all in passing as she headed straight for the bathroom.

Fresh and clean after a long, hot soak, Holly fixed a light supper and sat down to read her mail.

The letter on top was from Dr. Watson. Emmie must have recognized his handwriting and put it where Holly would see it first. Wondering what he'd be writing about, she slit open the envelope and withdrew the page.

Her eyes widened in surprise at the words written there.

Dr. Watson was offering to sell her part of his practice!

He wanted to slow down a bit, make more frequent visits to his children and grandchildren and wondered if she was interested in buying into partnership with him for the time being, with an option to buy the entire practice at a later date.

He'd heard some good things about her and was interested to know if she'd like such a deal.

Holly re-read the letter, unbelieving.

It was a generous offer, especially when she had never met the other vet personally, only by email, Skype and phone.

Who had he been talking to? Emmie? Cache?

It was a super opportunity. How many newly qualified vets had the chance to buy into an existing practice. One so crucial to the area?

Only…she paused and stared out of the window. She was returning to Kentucky.

If she didn't have that, she might consider staying in Redbud and accept Dr. Watson's offer.

For a moment she let herself indulge in daydreams, of her staying, Cache finding out and…

Enough of that. He'd made it clear that he wanted her sexually but not forever.

He was counting on her leaving. If she stayed, she'd bet he'd change his tune fast enough.

And she vowed she would never be like Sally Lambert, chasing after a man who didn't want her.

She slowly laid the letter aside and read the rest of her mail. But the offer stayed in the back of her mind.

The next morning she kept office hours. She was busy with dogs and cats and pet lambs. She'd been gone for over a week and as these patients weren't critically ill or injured their owners had decided to wait for her to return rather than visit

Stan Connors over in Overilla.

She remembered a few of the owners from the dance and chatted briefly with them. For a moment she considered what her life would be like if she stayed. It was nice to know people, to feel as if she belonged. As one of the town's vets, she'd have a place of respect. A sense of belonging. And she'd already made a start on it.

She used to belong at Windmere Farms. Once back there, she'd fit right in again.

It was after lunch when Holly heard the familiar truck in the driveway. She was glad she still wore the lab coat—it gave her a feeling of authority. And she needed every bit of it against the overwhelming magnetism of Cache McKendrick.

She walked to the door and waited for him as he walked up the path.

"Hello." She pushed open the screen and Cache stepped into the front room, immediately filling it with his presence.

Holly felt the familiar pull of attraction despite her feelings of the last few days of the drive.

"How're you doing? No lasting effects from the trip?"

He stopped close enough to her that Holly had to tilt her head back to see him, her lips tingling at the thought that he might kiss her. The beard was gone.

"I'm fine."

She stepped back, dropping her eyes lest he see the desire she guessed was displayed there. Why was he here?

"I wanted to see you."

He swept his hat off, running his fingers through his dark blond hair. It was a little long; he'd need to get it cut.

"Well, have a seat."

She sat down on one of the hardback chairs and watched him uneasily, conscious of all that had passed between them. She hadn't forgotten one single moment.

He eased himself onto the big overstuffed chair near the window and watched her. His eyes narrowed slightly as he studied her, taking in the soft flush to her cheeks, the vulnerability around her mouth, her hair pulled back for coolness, displaying her slender neck.

"I had a surprise when I got in last night," she said for something to say when the silence stretched out. "Dr. Watson has offered me a partnership."

Cache's eyebrow rose and he looked at her patiently. "And?"

"And nothing. I was surprised, that's all. You don't seem to be."

He shrugged, looked at his hat turning in his hands. He'd spoken to Doc Watson only a couple of weeks ago. Holly was good and he'd told him so. He hadn't known what the doc had in mind when he'd asked about Holly.

"Are you going to take up the offer?" he asked.

She shook her head slowly. "I have other plans, remember."

"I remember you saying that." His voice was neutral, his expression bland. "But are you sure of your reception?"

"I'm sure my uncle will be glad to see me. I'm hoping he'll let me work at Windmere Farms."

The uncertainty showed in her tone and she frowned.

He'd asked that before. Why was he throwing doubts on

her plans? What did he hope to accomplish? She didn't need to share her misgivings with Cache.

Uncle Tyson had been rigid in his decision before, but surely time would have mellowed him. The fact that she was a practicing vet should change his mind. It had to!

"Easy enough to find out. Why not call him? If there's no job there, you might want to consider Doc Watson's offer. No sense in burning bridges if you don't need to."

The suggestion sounded reasonable. Holly glanced at the phone for a moment then at Cache.

"Maybe. I'll see."

"Call now," he ordered.

She hesitated. Uncertain of her reception. What if her uncle refused to let her work for Windmere Farms? She wasn't sure a phone call would work. She'd planned to show up and convince him.

"I think I'll go visit. I can talk about it face to face to see how he feels."

After seven years, surely he'd at least listen to her. Give her a chance.

She'd proved she was up to the job. She'd made it this far on her own. Surely he'd see she had more to offer than play hostess at some fancy dinner.

"Doc probably wants an answer soon. Give your uncle a call, Holly."

Cache's eyes were dark blue, his jaw stubborn. Obviously a man used to being obeyed. That was how he built up his ranch, she thought. People listened to him.

"Fine."

She took a deep breath and went to dial the long-familiar number. Anticipation built. Should she have waited until evening? Ignore Cache's demand and fly home as originally planned?

Her uncle answered on the fourth ring. He was surprised to hear from her and the first few minutes of the conversation were a bit stilted spent in catching up.

When Holly broached the subject of her return, and possibly working at Windmere Farms, she was shocked at her uncle's response.

She could see Cache's attention as he carefully observed her reactions.

"I can't believe it…But Uncle Tyson…Yes, I understand that."

She was quiet a long time, listening to the voice on the line.

"Of course it's your decision. I'll write you about my job here. Tell the boys hi for me." Slowly she placed the receiver on its cradle blinking away the tears that had filled her eyes.

Turning to Cache, her eyes wide and shocked, she shook her head.

"How did you know?" she whispered.

"Know what?" He leaned forward, but remained seated his eyes taking in every nuance of her expression.

"There won't be a job at Windmere. There's not going to be a Windmere any more. He's selling it to Runningmede a rival farm. The two are merging."

Holly sank back in her chair, feeling numb.

"Uncle Tyson is retiring and plans to travel. He's

relinquishing the operations to the new owners."

For as long as she could remember she'd wanted to work with her uncle and cousins at Windmere Farms. Now that'd never be possible. She'd been gone too long. Left it too late. She couldn't believe it.

If she'd stayed in Kentucky, would the situation have been different?

Probably not.

She was never involved with the running of Windmere. She'd never have altered her uncle's thinking.

"Holly?"

Cache moved to hunker down beside her, taking her hands in his. They were like ice.

"Honey, are you okay?" His blue eyes mirrored his concern.

She nodded, gazing down at him, hurt and confusion obvious in her eyes.

"I'm just…numb, I guess. He sold the farm. He's retiring and going traveling–around the world. My cousins are set in their jobs. None of them wanted to take on the farm. I…it's the last thing I expected to hear."

She stared off into space, still unable to believe what her uncle told her.

He'd settle some money on her, he'd told her.

As if she had wanted anything like that. He still didn't understand her. She'd wanted to be a part of the family farm, have a part in working with the horses. Now she'd never get the chance.

"Hey, Holly, it's not the end of the world. There's always

Doc's offer." Cache said gently. "I think you should seriously think about it."

She stared at him. Cache would like her to stay around?

It'd only be a matter of time, then, before she succumbed to his pressure. She loved it when he kissed her, teased her, just spent time with her.

Then what?

Her hands tingled as he caressed the backs, his thumbs circling across her skin. She pulled them back. Time to end this before it led into something she couldn't handle. She needed time to think things through.

She felt as if the world had tilted on its axis. What was she going to do? All her thoughts for the future shattered. It'd take time to make sense of things.

To make new plans.

"I think you should go, Cache," she said softly. "I need to think about what I want to do."

She wanted to be alone. The reality was too much to take in at once. What if she hadn't called? Had arrived back home in five months and found no family there?

He rose and clamped his hat back on. "Let me know what you decide."

"I'm sure you'll hear." She rose and led the way to the door.

"Wait a minute; what do you mean?" he asked.

She looked up at him, her eyes wide with innocence.

"Why, only that if I stay you'll soon enough know it. The whole town gossips, doesn't it?"

"I'd rather hear it from you, darlin'."

Holly smiled. He didn't like someone holding back. He liked to be in charge.

But it was time he realized she for one didn't jump to his bidding. She realized her mistake when his eyes darkened and he lowered his head to hers.

She ducked away and pushed at him. "Please just leave, Cache. I have patients due here any minute."

The afternoon office hours were about to start. She didn't need to add any fuel to gossip. Especially if there was a chance of her staying on in Redbud.

"And I'd hate to start something I couldn't finish," he drawled.

"Right. Goodbye, Cache."

"Call me and let me know," he repeated.

She watched as he drove away, then closed the door wondering what she should do. What could she do? Was there any choice?

She had a job offer, a place she liked. And near that frustrating cowboy who disturbed her beyond belief. But was it enough?

Over the next several days Holly went about her work, assessing if Redbud was where she wanted to put down roots.

Or should she return to Kentucky and seek other opportunities there?

If her uncle would put in a good word for her, she bet she could find something with horses.

It was odd, after so long, to lose her goal. For years she'd planned to return home in triumph, winning the approval of her uncle and working at Windmere Farms. Another place wouldn't be the same.

Now she felt adrift, indecisive, mixed up. What should she do?

She needed to make some decision and move on. Right or wrong, something had to be decided and soon. Dr. Watson wanted an answer.

And she'd like to know where she'd be in the next year or two herself.

Friday she awoke with a decision made.

She'd stay in Redbud.

She'd call Dr. Watson today and accept his offer, then start looking for a place to live. By the time the Watsons returned home, she'd be ready to move to her new place.

She felt as if a weight had lifted—and wondered why she'd thought the decision so difficult.

Because of Cache.

Cache phoned and invited her over to go riding. She wasn't ready to face him.

Two days after making her decision and discussing things with Dr. Watson, she decided to let Cache know.

She wondered how he'd take the news. Anxiety and anticipation mixed. She wasn't sure she was ready for his reaction if it didn't go the way she hoped it would.

She hurried through her calls and prayed there'd be no emergencies. She didn't want to put off telling him, now that she'd decided to do so.

The day was breezy and a little cool when Holly set off for the ranch. She grabbed a sweatshirt before leaving home suspecting she'd need it before the day was over. Before long she turned into the driveway and reached the barn in short order.

It was quiet. A couple of horses in the corral dozed in the afternoon sun. Small dust whirlwinds jumped across the corral in the breeze.

The ranch seemed empty in the clear summer day. She got out, wondering if she should have called first.

"Howdy, Doc," Sam called from near the house. She smiled and waited as he hurried across the yard towards her.

"Hi, Sam, is Cache around?"

"Nope, he went out after breakfast, riding towards the west range, going to check on the cattle over there. He thought there might be a fence down somewhere. Should be back before too long. Want to wait?"

"Maybe I'll hang around for a little while."

She didn't want to make the trip a second time. Wiping her hands down her jeans, she tried to quell the butterflies in her stomach.

"Sally Lambert's up at the house. You could join her," he suggested.

Holly wrinkled her nose and shook her head.

"I don't think so. I'll check out Starlight and see how he's doing. See Beau. If Cache's not back by then, I'll come another time."

"You might take Tomahawk, catch him on the range."

Sam fell into step beside her as she entered the cool barn.

"Or I could miss him entirely—it's a wide open range and I'm not that familiar with it. It's not that important. I'll see him another time."

She certainly didn't want to tell Sam her news with Sally hanging around. What was she doing here anyway?

Would Cache think she was chasing him the way Sally did?

She should have waited and let him learn of her decision through the grapevine.

She crossed to the stall where the foal was housed and looked over the stall door at him. "He looks fine. He's eating well?"

She stroked his velvety muzzle when he ambled over to see her, his curiosity strong.

"Yeah, getting spoiled. Everyone watches out for him. Shame about his ma."

Sam rested his foot on the lower railing and watched the little horse.

"Cache bought that mare for Trish," she remembered.

"Yeah and Trish loved her. It was when they were first married and things were still okay. I think the boss always remembered the good days when he saw that mare."

"Cache told me Trish was leaving when she was killed," Holly said slowly, her fingers rubbing against the foal's head.

"Well, I wished she'd been killed a mite earlier," Sam said, his voice hard.

That surprised Holly. She swung around to stare at the old man.

"Why?"

"I wish she and her venomous tongue had gone long before they ruined a good man. Cache tried hard to make that marriage work. He gave her so much and she told him he couldn't make a woman happy. He took it to heart. He's never even looked at another woman. What this place needs is a woman and lots of kids."

"Hey, Sam, come quick," a panicked voice called from the yard.

Sam turned and ran from the barn, Holly right on his heels. She stopped at the door as one of the cowhands was trying to catch Roman. The big horse was lathered with sweat, his saddle empty.

"Where's Cache?" Holly heard Sam ask.

Her eyes were riveted to the saddle. Dark, rusty stains covered the side. The horse was cut, blood dripping from his side.

She hurried over and reached for one of the reins just as Sam got him under control.

"Don't know," said the cowhand. "I just saw Roman running and tried to get him."

Holly felt Roman's side. There were two gored areas, the blood flow already slowing. Her eyes were drawn again and again to blood on the saddle. Roman's blood hadn't flowed there.

"Blasted longhorn, I bet," Sam said. "I'll try to backtrack him. Frank, you call Doc Bellingham and tell him to stand by, we may need him."

"Wait, Sam, I want to come, too." Holly looked at the horse one more time. "Give me five minutes with Roman and I'll be ready.

If Cache was hurt, she wanted to be with him.

"Hurry, I'll saddle the horses. And bring your bag, Doc. Who knows what we'll find?" Sam hurried into the barn.

Holly ran to her truck and pulled out her bag. She followed the cowboy leading Roman into the barn. It took longer than five minutes, though it was a lick and a promise kind of help. She cleaned the wounds. Stitched one and placed a dressing over both to keep clean.

"Put him in a stall with clean shavings. Try to keep him from rolling," she instructed the cowboy.

Tossing the dirty bandages and gloves, she repacked the bag and dashed out to where Sam stood with the horses ready to go.

Holly tied her black bag on to the saddle and vaulted into the seat.

"He probably just got tossed," Sam said as they started out. Sam led the way at a gallop.

Holly hoped with all her heart that it was so.

Ten

Holly's heart pounded with fear as she and Sam followed the trail past the house and beyond. He seemed to know where he was going and she followed trusting he wanted to get to Cache as fast as she did.

Was he all right? Or was that his blood on the saddle? As they crested the ridge behind the homestead, Sam slowed a little and started looking at the ground, trying to see the direction Roman had come from. Holly trusted that the old cowboy knew what he was doing. She knew she'd never find Cache on her own.

She was fearful of what they would find, however. Cache was a good rider; to have fallen could mean he could be seriously injured. Or worse.

She remembered hitting her head when she fell. What if he'd injured himself even more?

She refused to let herself consider that. He had to be all right. She chanted that in her mind as they rode.

She followed Sam, staying behind him so as not to interfere, her own eyes searching the horizon, wanting to find Cache and assure herself he was okay. They'd probably find him walking along, cussing that old horse for dumping him.

And wouldn't she love to tease him about that.

She refused to think of anything worse.

Holly's throat ached and she had trouble swallowing. She couldn't imagine her world without Cache. He meant everything to her. With startling realization, she blinked.

She loved the man.

He was infuriating, patronizing and afraid to make a commitment to a woman. He was charming, a flirt and a teaser, but it didn't matter. She loved him!

He'd probably never love her, but she didn't care at that moment. Her life would be incomplete without him in it somehow. He had to be all right!

With that knowledge, it became more important than ever that they locate him. She had to make sure he was okay.

She was almost screaming with impatience and frustration as they continued to ride. Why couldn't Sam find him?

Her eyes searched the landscape looking for something out of the ordinary. Some sign of Cache.

But she saw only the bleached grass, the silvery sage, scattered rocks and the occasional live oak that dotted the range. In the distance, she could see cattle.

But no sign of her cowboy.

Where was he?

Time dragged. Minutes seemed endless as they slowed to study the ground. Here and there drops of blood were drying in the dirt. Sam drew up and studied the ground, pausing each time he found a drop of blood. Standing in his saddle he scanned the horizon. Searching for more signs, searching for Cache.

"I think I see him." Sam said after one such stop.

He spurred his horse and took off. Holly followed her eyes frantically trying to see what Sam had seen.

And there he was, leaning against a small boulder, leaning his head back, hat off and eyes closed. He didn't stir as the two rode up and hastily dismounted. Sam reached him first.

"Cache?"

Holly flung herself off her horse and stared at him. She was breathless, as if hit in the stomach. There was blood all over his left leg, soaking into the ground. An ineffective attempt had been made to staunch the flow using his bandanna. But blood still seeped out.

His hat was several feet away, too far for Cache to reach without some effort, and the blazing sun beat relentlessly down on his exposed face.

Holly's training took over. Quickly assessing the problem, she suspected that he had been gored by a longhorn, like his horse.

She glanced around quickly to see if the steer was still around, but saw nothing.

Yanking her bag off the saddle, she snatched up his hat in passing and hurried over to him.

Sam was testing for vital signs, looking at the leg.

"How is he?"

She knelt beside him, her heart pounding in fear; the pallor of his face was dreadful.

Please God, let him be alive!

"Pretty bad, I think. Look at all the blood. I'll ride for the ranch and call for the medevac helicopter. You stay with him, Doc." Sam looked at Holly, his eyes worried. "Can you do that? It'll be a while, but I don't want to leave him alone."

She nodded confidently. "I'll take good care of him. Hurry, Sam, but don't go getting hurt yourself on the way back."

She was already reaching for Cache's wrist as Sam mounted and started off pushing the horse for as much speed as it could deliver.

She sought a pulse. It was light, thready. His breathing was shallow. She knew he was in shock. Scrambling over to her horse, she snatched her sweatshirt from the saddle and hurried back. Each second seemed endless. Hurry, Sam, she urged.

While her heart was frantic with worry, she moved with calm efficiency. Laying Cache down on the rocky ground, she dragged a couple of flat rocks over to elevate his feet a little, covering him with the sweatshirt.

She set his hat gently on his head to shelter it from the sun and quickly opened her bag. There must be something she could do for him, if only to stop the bleeding.

When she looked back, he had his eyes opened, just a crack, but she was relieved to see he was conscious.

"Where else are you hurt?" she asked. "Besides your leg."

"I didn't expect you, darlin'." His voice was low, faint.

She nodded and tried to smile. Time to check the makeshift bandage he'd used. He had wadded up his bandanna to hold on his leg, but the pressure had eased when he fell unconscious.

"You've lost a lot of blood."

She cut away some of the jeans so that she could see the wound more clearly. The sun was hot on her back.

She felt small and lonely in the vast land with the injured man depending upon her. But her hands were steady and her voice firm. She was a professional and could keep her personal feelings from showing when the task demanded it.

"Feel light-headed," he mumbled, his eyes riveted on her.

"I don't wonder. Hold still; I want to see if–"

She examined the wound, appalled at the amount of blood still flowing. The wound was ragged, a bit dirty and the blood-flow wasn't slowing. It looked as if the steer had nicked an artery.

She bit her lip and looked at him in indecision.

"Cache, you're still bleeding pretty bad. How long ago did this happen?" She pressed a pad to the wound, leaning against him to apply pressure, trying desperately to staunch the flow.

"Don't know. Tried to make it home with Roman. He's hurt too. Blacked out, I guess. Fix me up, darlin"."

"I'm a horse doctor, not a people doctor."

The pad was slowly turning bright red.

"An artery is an artery whether you're a horse or a man. Holly, if you don't do something I could bleed to death." His voice sounded weaker.

She nodded, knowing that was probably true. She glanced around in despair at the blood already soaking into the thirsty ground. How much had he already lost? S

he checked her watch. Sam wouldn't even be at the ranch

yet. How much longer before she could expect the medevac helicopter?

She glanced at him again. His breathing was shallow. Her mind raced. She knew she had to do something to save him. But dared she?

Reaching a decision, she turned to her bag and drew out the sutures from her case. Her hands shook slightly, but she knew he was right. The bleeding had to stop or he'd die.

She cut more of the jeans around the wound, high up on his thigh, and heard him chuckle. She glanced up, met his eyes, marveling that he could find anything amusing at this time.

Her heart turned over when her eyes locked with his. She loved him so much she ached with it!

"I wanted…to get your pants…off, never thought of…you cutting mine…off."

She gave him a speaking glance and filled a syringe with Xylocaine. The man had a one-track mind.

"I don't know about this, Cache. I know how to do it for large animals. This will numb the area for the sutures. Anyway, I don't want to wait any longer."

She was proud of her firm voice. She didn't want to frighten him. And she sure hoped she wouldn't lose her license because of this. Surely in an emergency any help was better than none.

"Hey, one animal's…pretty much the same as any…other. Anyway, I think you're…right not to wait."

Was his voice getting weaker?

Holly administered the local anesthetic, waited a minute for it to take effect, then began closing the wound. She found the source of the bleeding and sutured it closed. Her hands were steady, her mind occupied with the work at hand.

She refused to dwell on the fact it was Cache she was working on.

Nor of the ramifications should anyone press charges. She was a vet, for God's sake, not a physician.

But if she didn't do this, he'd die, she was sure of it.

He passed out before she finished. She continued working, competently and efficiently, refusing to think about his losing consciousness again. Refusing to think of anything except the procedure at hand. She closed off the nick in the artery, closing the wound and packed it in bandages.

When finished, she sank back on the ground, her hands soaked with his blood, trembling now that the procedure was finished. She swallowed a couple of times and looked up to clear her eyes of the tears that threatened.

She prayed she'd done everything right. "Please don't let him die," she breathed.

"Cache?" she called his name softly.

She felt for his pulse; it was slow, weak. His breathing was steady, however.

She cleaned her hands as best she could with the wipes in her case.

"Come on, Cache, wake up."

She brushed the hair from his forehead, her fingers trailing through the thickness. He was so still. She felt for his pulse again.

"Cache, don't you die on me, do you hear me, cowboy?"

Fear rose like bile in her throat.

He lay so still. She checked again to make sure he was still breathing.

"Cache, wake up. Don't you dare die on me." Tears welled up and she impatiently dashed them away. "Please don't go. I love you. Please be all right. I'm staying in Redbud. So you better be here for me. Do you hear me? Oh, Cache, please hear me."

"I hear you, darlin'." His voice was faint, his eyes remained closed. "No good staying–"

"Of course it is. I'll be the best vet this town ever saw. Stay with me, Cache."

Her hands held his tightly. Her strength willed him to stay conscious.

Where was that helicopter? She scanned the sky, saw nothing.

"Don't love me, Holly," he said, his eyes opening a slit.

"I can love whomever I want. You can't boss everyone."

This was so not how she ever expected to tell him her feelings. Actually, she hadn't expected to tell him at all.

"Never work–" He closed his eyes.

"You don't know that. I'm not Trish. Think on it, Cache. I'm not Trish and you can't lump us together. I've lived here for weeks now and know all about the small town, the ranches and ranchers in the county. I'm not going to pine for the city, for shopping and nightclubs and traveling. I've been on cattle drives. Love the feeling of belonging I get when talking with neighbors or others I've met since I've been here. Trish and I aren't anything alike. You're just being stubborn. Do you love me?"

He was silent.

"Oh, my love, don't die, hold on, Sam's gone for help, hold on. It'll be okay."

She cradled his hand in hers, hugging it to her breasts, willing life into him, willing him to hold on and not die.

"Yes." The word was whispered.

Yes what? Yes, he loved her? Or yes, he'd hold on?

She kissed his hand. He had to live, he simply had to!

She loved him so much and she wanted him to love her. But if he didn't, she still needed him to live, to be a part of her life.

She glanced at his leg; the bandages were still white; thank God the bleeding stopped. But he'd lost so much blood. Would he make it?

She couldn't bear it if he died.

Where was that blasted helicopter?

"Roman?"

She looked at him. He was hovering near death and was worried about his horse.

"He's fine or will be. Frank's watching him. I checked him before we left the ranch. A few stitches. He'll recover."

She kept her tone positive. She didn't want him worrying about the horse. She hoped the time she'd taken for his horse hadn't made a difference in Cache's chances of recovery. How much blood had he lost? The ground around them seemed soaked with it.

Tears slid down her cheeks. She was so afraid. So alone and afraid. It was a big country, needing strong people to live in it. She felt insignificant.

He opened his eyes a little, a small smile tugging at his lips. "Your…bedside manner leaves a lot to be desired. The last time…you cried was when a horse died…Am I dying?"

She brushed at her tears with the back of one hand, still clasping his against her breast. She shook her head.

"No, you're not. You're too stubborn to die from some dumb old cow."

"Steer, darlin'', goldarn ornery old longhorn steer." For a moment his voice had a familiar teasing ring.

"I knew that," she whispered, her hand gripping him, delighted that he could answer back.

He had to recover. She scanned the sky again. Nothing.

"You're so pretty, honey. You should be…doing teas and going to the opera…to dances." His voice was getting softer. He spoke more slowly.

She shook her head, tears still slipping down.

"Not my thing. like Grange dances and camping out, and riding hard and fast. I like the open range land of California and small towns where the people like you if you do your job well."

She looked up. She heard something. The whomp whomp of the helicopter. She searched the sky. There, she saw it coming over the hill and flying low.

"Help's almost here, Cache," she said excitedly.

"You're my help," he mumbled before falling unconscious again.

In only a couple of moments the big med-evac helicopter settled down some distance away, its blades slowing as it kicked up dust and rocks. Before the blades fully stopped, two paramedics jumped down and hurried over to Holly. Sam was right behind them.

In less than two minutes, Holly and Cache were lifting off in the helicopter and Sam was riding her horse back to the ranch. Holly squeezed into the corner of the helicopter and watched as the paramedics administered plasma and took Cache's vital signs. She wanted some indication from the men that Cache would be okay, but she could tell nothing from their sporadic conversation.

It was out of her hands now. She could only pray she'd done enough.

Dr. Bellingham met the helicopter at the county hospital. He greeted Holly and directed her to the nearby waiting room, his attention all for Cache.

She sank down in one of the chairs, noticing for the first time the blood on her jeans and shirt. Cache's blood. Slowly she rose and found a washroom to clean up. It all seemed unreal.

Only, she knew it wasn't.

Was he going to be all right? He hadn't regained consciousness in the helicopter.

The wait was endless. After a while she was joined by Sam. But she didn't know how long she sat there. He brought her some coffee and she sipped at it for something to do. Her heart and soul were in limbo until she heard how Cache was doing.

Dr. Bellingham walked into the waiting room, a big smile on his face. He nodded to Sam and spoke to Holly.

"Well, if Doc Watson doesn't want you for a partner,

come see me. You did a fine job on Cache. Saved his life, I reckon. Another pint of blood gone and he'd be dead."

"But he's okay now?"

"I think he will be. We pumped a little blood in him, checked him over. We'll know better in the morning. We'll monitor his vitals all night. Go home, Holly. You did a good thing, but there's nothing further to be done. You can come back and see him in the morning."

The doctor's voice was gentle, his smile kindly but his tone firm.

She might as well go home. She nodded, feeling drained and exhausted.

"I'll give you a ride home, Doc," Sam said, twisting his hat in his hand.

"No, take me to the ranch first, Sam. I want to check Roman to make sure he's doing okay," Holly said.

She'd promised Cache. Besides, her truck was there.

It was after midnight by the time Holly reached home. Roman had required a change of bandages. His stitches were holding and he hadn't tried to roll at all, so the cowboy watching him said. She'd instructed the cowhands to keep him in the stall for a few days. He'd be fine by then.

She only hoped Cache would heal as quickly.

She was utterly exhausted. She drove home carefully, fighting to keep awake.

Holly held off until she was in bed, but then gave way to the tears of relief that had threatened since Dr. Bellingham had said Cache would recover.

Over and over she relived the fear of the afternoon, the

fear when she'd seen him so unlike his normal robust, sexy self.

The doctor said he'd be fine. She had to hold on to that. The tears flowed for a long time.

Holly spent a restless night and awoke early. She waited impatiently until eight o'clock when she could call the hospital.

The nurse who answered informed her that Cache had spent a comfortable night and the doctor was with him now. She hadn't yet heard if the doctor was permitting visitors. Perhaps Holly could check back later?

Holly hung up the phone, certain that Dr. Bellingham would let her see Cache. He'd as much as promised last night. She'd wait for Emmie, tell her what had happened and then go to the hospital.

Holly ate a hasty breakfast and was washing the dishes when the phone rang. Thinking it was Dr. Bellingham, she dashed to grab it before the second ring, anxious to hear the latest about Cache.

"Holly, Stan Connors, vet over at Overilla. I've got a problem and need your help."

"What's up?"

Her eyes glanced impatiently at the clock. Almost nine; Emmie should be here soon. She'd update Emmie and then leave for the hospital.

"...so I'm not sure but I think it's anthrax."

Holly's attention quickly turned to what Stan was saying. She'd missed the first part, but her attention was caught by the dreaded word anthrax. The disease could go through a herd in no time, wiping it out, spreading to neighboring ranches before you knew it.

"Tell me again," she said, her attention fully on Stan.

He was unsure, but the symptoms sounded classic. He wanted her help in isolating the animals, analyzing the disease and taking steps to make sure it didn't spread if it were anthrax.

"I'm on my way," she said, her mind spinning with everything she needed to take.

They'd studied this in school, of course. But she never thought she'd have any contact with the disease.

She hoped Emmie would arrive before she left. She needed to tell her about Cache, see if she'd go and visit Cache for her, explain why she couldn't come herself today.

It wasn't satisfactory, but it'd have to do, Holly thought a short time later when she was driving over to Overilla to meet Stan. She wanted to see for herself that Cache was all right, but she trusted Dr. Bellingham to do his job as she had to do hers.

For four days Holly worked harder than she'd ever done. She and Stan did indeed find anthrax in some of the cattle recently purchased from a herd in Mexico. Harry Barnard, the rancher with the affected cattle, was afraid the disease would spread to his healthy cattle.

By the end of four days, they'd isolated all infected animals and put them down. Biohazard cleanup was underway.

The rest of the herd was inoculated. The pasture where the new herd had grazed closed until it could be sanitized—an expensive and time-consuming project.

Fortunately Stan caught the disease in time to prevent major damage to Barnard's herd, and prevented spread to any other ranches in the county.

As a precaution, Barnard's herd would be kept in isolation for a few weeks, but the worst was behind them.

The calls had been non-stop once the word spread and Emmie and Dr. Connors" assistant spent long hours on the phone reassuring everyone.

This was cattle country it was natural that everyone was concerned about the threat of anthrax.

When Holly reached home the night of the fourth day, she checked her desk for the messages Emmie left her on Cache's progress. It was her only link to him. She'd risen early each day, been gone until after dark.

He'd been asleep when she'd called the first night. After that, she hadn't tried, but relied on the notes that Emmie left for her. It hadn't been satisfactory, but she'd had no choice.

"Cache is fine," Emmie had written.

Holly shook her head and headed for bed. She'd have liked a little more than a cryptic note, but Emmie didn't know that. It was a frustrating way to keep up with his recovery but Holly didn't have a better one.

The next morning she called the hospital, hoping to talk to Cache.

"Oh, Dr. Murphy, Cache checked out yesterday afternoon. He's home now," the cheerful voice said.

Holly's spirits lightened. She'd see to her patients and then go out to visit him. He must be doing better for Dr. Bellingham to have released him.

Because she'd been essentially gone for almost a week, the backlog of patients was long. It was late when she finished, too late to drive to the Lone Tree and visit a convalescing cowboy.

Frustration was driving her wild.

Tomorrow, sick animals or not, she was going to see Cache!

The next afternoon, calling a halt to her rounds, she stopped in town for a bouquet of flowers, then headed to the Long Tree Ranch.

She couldn't believe it was six days since she'd last seen him. Six endless days. She needed to reassure herself he was mending. She wanted to listen to his teasing, have him kiss her.

She couldn't wait for him to kiss her again. Surely he'd give her at least one kiss. If only for saving his life.

When she stopped to her normal parking spot near the barn, she saw the pickup Sally Lambert drove.

Her heart sank. Was she here?

Taking a deep breath, Holly gathered her flowers and walked to the house.

The day was warm, the sun bright in a cloudless blue sky, and the scent of cattle, hot dust and the sage from the hills mingled to remind Holly of the cattle drive, the rides she and Cache had made, the fright she'd had the day she and Sam had found him so badly injured.

Sally must have seen her drive up. She came to the door and slipped through before Holly stepped up on the porch.

"Cache is resting now. I'll tell him you stopped by," she said, blocking the entrance.

"I could wait," Holly said, still holding the flowers in front of her.

"I wouldn't if I were you. He could sleep for hours. Do you want me to call you when he wakes up?" Sally asked.

Holly stared at her, then smiled. "Would you?"

Sally shrugged. She reached for the flowers. "No point in waiting."

"You're waiting," Holly said.

"Actually, Dr. Murphy, I've been helping out since he got home. You're an outsider to our community. You might not realize how we all rally around to help each other out in emergencies. Cache and I have something special between us so of course I help out when needed. He knows where you live. If he'd wants to see you, he can call or send one of the men."

Holly stared at her for a moment, struck by what Sally said.

She nodded and gave up, her heart sinking.

Much as she hated to admit it, Sally was right. Cache had been well enough to go home yesterday. If he'd wanted to talk to her, he could have called.

Her face burned with embarrassment. She gave a polite smile and felt as if her face would crack. Cache was probably glad she hadn't come by.

How awful to have someone say they love you if you didn't love them back.

"I'll check on Roman, then, and be off. Do tell him I came to see him," she said, knowing the chances of that were probably slim.

But did it really matter? Cache had never indicated that he wanted anything more than a casual fling. He thought she'd be leaving for Kentucky. Now she was staying.

How awkward for him.

She handed the flowers to Sally and turned to walk back to the barn.

She hoped he didn't remember her babbling when he'd been so injured. She'd like to forget it, pretend it never happened. Otherwise, she wasn't sure she could remain in Redbud.

Cache didn't want to make any kind of commitment to a woman. And if he ever changed his mind, why look further than Sally Lambert? He'd known her all her life, knew what kind of wife she'd make, knew she was used to a rancher's life. She wouldn't long for the city as Trish had done.

Even that day on the range, Cache had told Holly she should go back to dances and teas. As if that interested her.

He didn't know her at all if he thought she'd be satisfied with that lifestyle. Her spirits dropped a little lower.

She found the barn deserted, except for Starlight in one stall and Roman in the adjacent one.

"Hi, guys," she said softly, glad to see both doing so well. She slipped into Roman's stall to examine him. He was doing fine, almost healed. Sam or the other cowboys had been taking care of him.

Then she stepped into the next stall to visit Starlight. He was growing despite the loss of his mother. Cache was doing something right, the foal was flourishing. She watched him for a few moments, her spirits lightened a little bit by his antics. He was so adorable.

Time was passing and there was nothing more for Holly

to do. She left the barn and slowly headed for the truck.

"Holly!"

She turned. Cache was crossing the ground from the house, swinging along on crutches. Holly stared and a smile started when she saw him. Slowly she walked towards him, her eyes never leaving his. He'd obviously dressed hastily—he was barefoot, jeans on and zipped, a shirt drawn on but not buttoned.

Her heart began beating heavily in her chest as she walked to the man she loved.

Eleven

"How are you doing?" Holly asked.

She was glad to see him up and about. He'd been so close to death. Now he looked as cocky as ever. She couldn't help smiling broadly.

He stopped and rested on the crutches, his eyes blazing blue down at her, taking in the soft brown hair, the brandy colored eyes gazing back at him so trustingly. His lips tilted in his lop-sided grin.

"I'm doing fine. Should be riding again in a day or two."

The soft drawl was music to Holly's ears.

"No. It's too soon."

He chuckled. "You're right, it'll be a few weeks, according to Doc Bellingham."

"I should hope so! But not according to you?"

She knew him. A few weeks would be too long. He'd chafe at the inactivity.

"Hey, I'm up, walking and doing fine. A week or so's all I need to get back to normal."

"I was so afraid–"

She stopped. Reaching out to touch him, she ran her hand

lightly down his arm, feeling the heat of him through the light cotton of the shirt, as if her touch could reassure her that he was alive and would be fine. Her eyes were drawn to his chest revealed through the open shirt. She felt herself fight the longing to rest her head against him, to be drawn into his arms, to feel his lips on hers again.

"Cache, what are you doing out of bed? Dr. Bellingham said you needed bed rest."

Sally came hurrying out of the house and down the path like an irate nurse.

"I'm fine, Sally, don't hover," he said without looking away from Holly.

When Sally reached them she glared at Holly then turned to Cache, her features softening.

"Come on back inside, Cache. She can come in to visit if you're up to it."

"I'm up to it."

His eyes were still fixed on Holly. She felt as if she was drowning in the sensations, the deep blue gaze holding her as if he'd never let her go.

"Run along, Sally, this is grown-up stuff," Cache said as the girl hovered near by.

"Cache."

She looked at Holly, her eyes angry, but bafflement soon replaced anger.

"I appreciate your help, Sally. And your dad's. But I've got someone who can help me now in ways you never could." He raised an eyebrow at Holly. "Right?" he asked softly.

She nodded, too afraid to speak.

Was he saying what she wanted to hear or was she imagining things?

Sally waited a moment then left, but neither Holly nor Cache noticed.

"I owe you my life, Doc Bellingham said," he said, shifting slightly on the crutches.

She shrugged. "I'm glad I was able to do something. I was so afraid that day. You lost a lot of blood, you know."

She didn't want to be talking about that awful day. She wanted to hear more about why he'd sent Sally away. And how she could help him in ways Sally never could.

"Yeah, and much as I hate to admit it, Sally's right—I need to get back inside."

Holly giggled slightly, relieved that the tension was easing.

"I should think so, rushing out here barefoot and half dressed. Weren't you in bed?"

"Yes, but when I heard your voice, I knew you were here and I wanted to see you. Sally wasn't exactly encouraging. I didn't have time to waste. Weren't you ready to leave?"

"You could have called me. I would have come back out," she said gently.

She walked with him back up the path and held the screen door open for him. With a quick glance around, she saw Sally pulling away the dust kicked up behind her truck drifting on the still air before settling back on the baked earth.

Cache sank on the sofa and tossed the crutches down with a clatter.

"A few more days and I won't need them, but the good

doctor doesn't want the stitches to pull out. Your stitches, as I hear."

Holly sat gingerly near him on the sofa, watching warily. Tension began to build and she wondered what he was going to say.

He leaned back and watched her, his eyes narrowed.

"Want to tell me why this is the first time I've seen you since the day of the accident?" he said, his voice calm and even.

But Holly wondered at the slight tightening of his lips.

She tried not to let her hopes rise too much at his question, wanting to launch herself into his arms, cover him with kisses and have him tell her he loved her. Of course she couldn't. He'd never given her any reasons to suspect he felt the same way she did. He'd been up front about merely wanting an affair.

"Didn't Emmie tell you?" she asked.

He shook his head. "I haven't seen Emmie. I haven't had any visitors, except Sam. And Sally. I wasn't really feeling up to it."

"Emmie told me each day you were doing better. I thought that meant she talked to you. Never mind that. I was over at Overilla, helping Stan. There was an outbreak of anthrax." She looked at him, so glad he was on the mend.

He whistled softly, his face grim. "Bad?"

"No, we caught it early. Harry Barnard lost fifty head all told. He'd just bought some cattle from Mexico and they were infected. We isolated them, put them down and the hazmat folks took care of them. Then we inoculated his cattle and the herds on the range adjoining his land. I wanted to come see you at the hospital, but it was way too late each night by the time I got home. Then when I finally did call the hospital you'd already been discharged. So here I am." She smiled shyly, trying to gauge his reaction.

Had he heard her that day? Would he let her down easily? Or be blunt as he'd been with Sally?

"Holly, out on the range you said you loved me. In fact, you were quite specific about loving me and that I was not to die."

His eyes held hers, amusement lurking in their depths at the memory.

She closed her eyes in embarrassment. His finger tapped her chin, and she opened her eyes to stare into his. The laughter was gone; they were serious as he looked at her.

"Remember what I told you, that after Trish I didn't want to try that route again?"

"I remember."

She blinked, trying to keep the tears at bay. She'd confessed her love and he was reminding her that he wouldn't be tied to a woman again. She felt the ache in her heart and wished she could push it away.

Why had she come today? Nothing had changed. He was the same as always. And he had always been honest with her.

"So was it just the heat of the moment? Why did you tell me that, Holly?" he asked.

"Because that's how I feel," she whispered, unable to lie about it.

"Oh, darlin'."

Cache reached out for her and drew her close, putting one arm around her shoulders and tilting her head up for a kiss.

She'd wanted him to kiss her for ages, but not like this—not out of pity!

His lips teased hers as he deepened the kiss his tongue caressing her plunging in her waiting mouth to bring her the satisfaction she knew he alone could give her.

She pushed against him. She wanted to escape with some pride still intact.

He pulled back after a moment, staring down at her, puzzled. He moved to take her in his arms again, but she pushed against his chest, ignoring the flame of desire that curled within her at the contact of his bare skin against her hands.

"Don't, you'll pull your stitches," she protested, afraid he'd injure himself again, yet not willing to stay within his embrace.

"Something tells me I'm as close to getting what I want as I've ever been and I still can't have you."

"What is it you want, Cache? To sleep with me?"

"Darn straight on that, darlin'."

He dropped a swift kiss on her mouth.

"For the memories?"

Exciting memories, wasn't that what he'd said? She held on to her tenuous control. She needed to get out, before she broke down completely. She blinked her eyes again. Judging the distance to the door.

"For the sheer pleasure of it, darlin'. Don't you want me?"

She looked up at him, unable to deny it. She loved him so much she'd give almost anything to sleep with him every night. To wake up with him each day and for them to spend their lives together, sharing, planning, loving, growing old together.

"Memories aren't enough," she said slowly, wondering if she should take what he offered. Afraid that would lead to greater heartbreak down the road.

"We'll have some grand ones to look back on when we're old and gray. Not that I plan to stop making them just because we get old."

She looked at him, puzzled.

"You know, the Chinese have a saying that if someone saves your life, that life's theirs," he said.

"You don't owe me anything."

How awful if he felt obligated to her. Her heart squeezed at the thought.

"I think I'm making a mess of this and that wasn't my intention. Actually, seeing you today threw me off. I thought I could plan this better."

"What?"

"I remember how I felt when you said you loved me. I was half out of my head with pain, and loss of blood I guess. I wanted to deny it, to deny how I felt about you. You were leaving, so I thought. It was safe to love you a little when I knew you'd be going. Then it all changed and you were staying—and making a strong case why I should consider you and me together."

Holly watched him, afraid to let her hopes rise.

"I keep remembering Trish. What I feel for you isn't like

what I felt for Trish."

Holly's heart died a little. She didn't have to be told that.

"Hey." He saw the hurt in her eyes. "What I feel for you is stronger, deeper. I'm older now, and know myself better. I love you, Holly, more than life itself. If you don't stay and marry me, I'll just give up. It hurt that I couldn't make a good marriage with Trish. But we just weren't right for each other. I swore off women because of a failed marriage, but looking back I think that was mainly my pride. It's a risk, but a chance I'm willing to take, if you are, darlin'. If you don't marry me, I'll die, darlin', just shrivel up and die. We could have a good marriage, Holly, I know it."

Holly couldn't believe her ears. Had he asked her to marry him?

"Holly?"

"Oh, Cache, I love you!"

She flung her arms around his neck, reached up eagerly for his kiss, all thoughts of his injuries forgotten.

"You still didn't answer me," he said whimsically a few minutes later.

Not wanting to stop, he had to nevertheless, before he ignored the doctor's advice and did something to cause damage to his stitches.

"You really didn't ask me anything," she said, her smile mischievous, her heart pounding with her audacity.

"Holly Murphy, will you do me the honor of becoming my wife?"

"Cache McKendrick, the honor would be all mine. Yes! Are you sure?"

"Darlin'", I've been sure since the first day I met you, with those indecent shorts and your feisty attitude. I remember hoping fervently that you weren't the interim vet's wife. But I wasn't sure about taking a second chance at the marriage route."

"Hah! At least I wasn't some arrogant cowboy, going around calling everyone "darlin'"" when I first met them."

"But you were my darling, even that first day. You're the only one I've ever called that, darlin'". Not even Trish was as darling as you are."

"You kept saying you'd never get married again. Why the change of heart? Not that I'm complaining."

She kissed him shyly on the corner of his mouth.

He settled back against the cushions and threaded his fingers through hers, watching their linked hands for a moment.

"It was that dern steer. When Roman took off after we were attacked, I really wondered if I'd make it. I thought about you. What if I never saw you again?"

He closed his eyes briefly, then glanced at her.

"Then I woke up there you were crying and telling me you loved me. I couldn't believe it. Once in the hospital, I had doubts. Had I imagined it all? You didn't come, didn't call, didn't try to see me. Maybe it'd been a hallucination. It didn't matter. That fear of death had me looking at life differently. I knew I wanted you more than anything ever. I vowed the next time I saw you I'd find out for sure how you felt and let you know I love you. And that I'm finally brave enough to take a chance to share my life with you."

Holly's heart glowed with love. Her long-time dreams no longer held any hold on her. They'd been replaced with even better ones. Sharing a practice in a town that was friendly and sharing her life with a man who loved her.

She'd found love with Cache McKendrick. Together they'd work on the Lone Pine ranch, raise a family to love the land and follow in their father's footsteps. And maybe one or two who would follow in their mother's footsteps.

She could envision their life and it filled her with delight.

She smiled, snuggling closer. "So, cowboy, when did you want to get married?"

He looked at his watch and she laughed.

"Not until I'm healed, that's for sure," he said.

She nodded. She imagined their wedding night, her heart tripping faster in excitement.

"You'll have to call your uncle, catch him before he starts on that trip around the world if he wants to give you away. My mother's going to be over the moon. She always wanted a daughter."

"I haven't even met your parents. What if they don't like me?" she asked, suddenly filled with doubts.

"Darlin'' they'll love you. But even if they didn't who cares, I love you. That's what counts in my life."

She nodded. Her arrogant cowboy was right again. His love was all that counted for her. New dreams and goals awaited. She couldn't wait to see what the future held for them–together.

If you liked **Second Chance Cowboy**,
you'll love the next book in the *Cowboy Hero* series,
Movie Star Cowboy.

If you enjoyed **Second Chance Cowboy**
please consider leaving a review.

More Books by Barbara McMahon

Cowboy Hero Series
The Cowboy Next Door
Cowboy's Bride
One Stubborn Cowboy
Crazy About a Cowboy
Never Doubt a Cowboy
Cowboy Marshal
Summer Cowboy
Second Chance Cowboy
Movie Star Cowboy

Cowboys of Wildcat Creek
Valentine's Cowboy Rescue
Shelly and the Cowboy
Kristi's Cowboy Hero
Holly's Reluctant Cowboy
A Cowboy for Eliza

Sweet Reunion Romance Collection
Unexpected Reunion
Unpredictable Reunion
Unanticipated Reunion

The Harts of Texas Series
Rebel Heart
Tangled Hearts
Reckless Heart

Ultimate Billionaires Series
The Cynical Sheikh
Falling for the Sheikh
A Sheikh of Her Own
The Unforgettable Sheikh

Rocky Point Series
Rocky Point Legacy
Rocky Point Reunion
Rocky Point Promise
Rocky Point Hero
Rocky Point Inn
Rocky Point Dawn

The Talmadge Sisters Series
Letters to Caroline
Michelle's Marriage Deal
Trusting Abby

Tropical Escapes Series
Island Rendezvous
Come into the Sun
Island Paradise

A Sweet Clean Christmas Romance Collection
The Christmas Cop
The Cowboy's Special Christmas
A Soldier's Christmas
A Teaspoon of Mistletoe
The Christmas Locket
A Key West Christmas

Sweet Romance Stand-alone Collection
Because of You
Cowboy Charade
I'll Take Forever
Jared's Promise
Mail Order Bride
Not Really Married
Sweet Meant To Be
The Cowboy Comes Home
The Paper Marriage
Trusting Jake
The Banished Bride